"What it is......"

by

S. Ashdown

Copyright © 2015 Samantha Ashdown
All rights reserved.
ISBN 10: 1511900318
ISBN-13: 9781511900317

For Ben and Mum

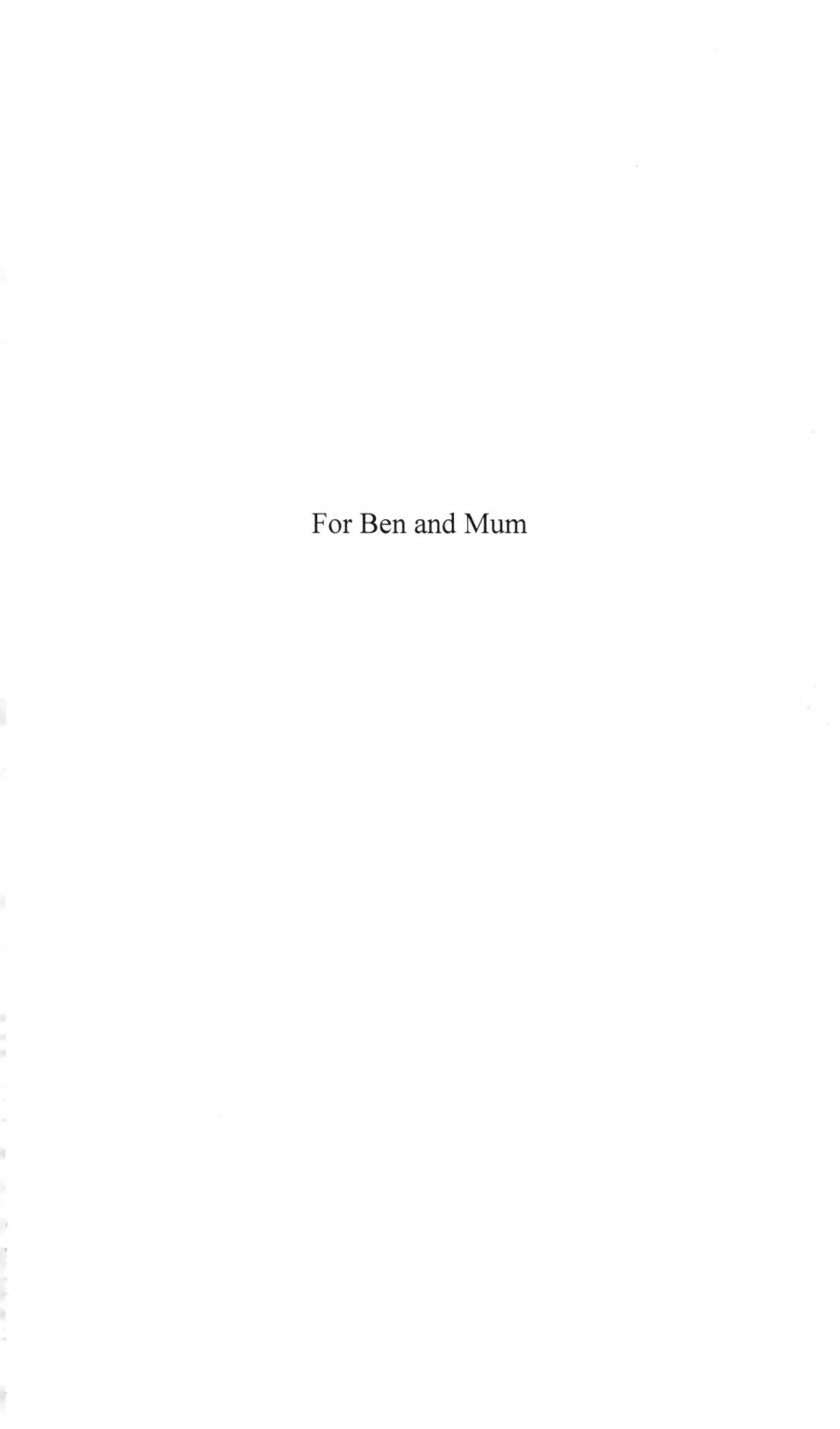

Chapter 1

'Thank goodness for that', thought Jasmine as the clock struck eight o'clock in the evening. She turned the key to lock the automatic doors at the front of the police station where she worked, turned the foyer lights off, locked the front door using the auto key that was behind the front counter and turned the blinds down. She turned the office lights off and was in the process of shutting her computer down when there was a loud bang on the front door of the police station. Jasmine ducked down behind the desk as whoever it was might see her shadow through the glass door to the office. Someone banged again.

'Bugger off', she muttered under her breath.

The computer had shut down and she turned the desktop police radio off whilst on her knees. She grabbed her handbag and crawled on her hands and knees out of the front office and into the back office, which was out of sight of the front door. She stood up, brushed the bits of floor dirt from her black uniform trousers and put on her warm and cosy duffle coat. It was almost the end of October and as usual the weather in the Welsh valley town, where she lived and worked, was cold, wet and windy and quite miserable.

Jasmine crept out of the Police station into the back yard so the person who had been banging on the front door didn't hear her.

"What is the matter with them", she muttered under her breath. She was annoyed as the station was open from eight o'clock in the morning until eight o'clock at night, seven days a week, there was a huge sign on the door and people always seemed to choose to go to the station just at closing time. She tutted to herself. Ordinarily she would have opened it and dealt with whatever crisis or document production and verification was so inconveniently needed, but not today, no-way, enough was enough.

She had been in the office by herself all day with only the visitors to the front desk to speak to. No-one had bothered to cover for her to have a break, and had to eat her lunch between phone calls and dealing with people at the desk, and no-one bothered to check to see if she needed anything, so she thought 'SOD IT'. Normally it was the role of her Sergeant to arrange cover but he had been off on a course somewhere and there wasn't anyone else to help her.

Another reason why she didn't answer the door was that she was going on her holiday early the next morning. She hadn't been abroad or had a proper holiday of sorts for five years and nothing and no-one was going to stop her. She had re-opened the door once before just as she had closed up, and had to deal with a man who wanted to hand himself in as he had smashed a shop window because he was homeless and wanted somewhere warm and dry to stay for the night. She ended up waiting hours for a police officer to return back to the station as there had been a three vehicle road traffic collision and all resources had been tied up dealing with it.

She had been away for the odd long weekend with friends but only to somewhere in Britain, all very nice, but it wasn't the same as going abroad, going on a plane and then endless lazing in the sunshine whilst sipping cocktails and occasionally turning over to even out the tan.

Jasmine had booked a much wanted, much needed holiday to Hawaii. A few weeks away from the constant, "What it is...is", that everyone seemed to say when they either went to the police station or rang the police station to complain about their lives that mostly compared to that of the guests on the 'Jeremy Kyle show.'

She had saved and scrimped and squirrelled away money for a few years. She had dreamed of going to Hawaii ever since she could remember. She loved the cheesy Elvis films, 'Blue Hawaii' and 'Paradise, Hawaiian style". She watched the whole series of 'Lost', not having a clue what the hell was going on, just because it was filmed on the paradise island of Oahu. She had also recorded every series of the new version of Hawaii five-o on Sky TV and she had even had a tattoo on her foot of Hawaiian hibiscus flowers. She wanted the tattoo to symbolise her close family, like they did on 'Miami ink'. Jasmine didn't have a sad story like they did in the TV show, just that she loved everything about Hawaiian culture so she had four large, aqua blue flowers to symbolise her mum, her teenage son, her brother and her grandmother. She had two very small white flowers to symbolise her beloved collie cross dog, Ruby, and her raggedy old cat,

Bridget. You could say she was overly obsessed with everything Hawaiian! Although she wasn't fussed on Hawaiian pizza.

Jasmine got into her little convertible, black Mini which was parked in the rear yard of the police station. She called her mini her 'Lickle Lilliputia', but not out loud in front of strangers! She had heard the word 'Lilliputia' in a World War Two mini-series on TV about the war in the Pacific, which she had watched the previous summer when she was off work after having a knee operation to reset a dislocated knee cap which was caused by a fall. She had thought it was one of the best series she had ever seen on TV and didn't want it to end. Not normally a fan of World War Two or any war stuff, but this was amazing. It was about the US marines out in the Pacific islands and their gruelling fight against the ruthless Japanese soldiers. They had used the word 'Lilliputia' as a code word as the Japanese had trouble saying it. Jasmine was fascinated by this word and looked it up in the dictionary, as she always did when she saw or heard a word that she hadn't heard before, and only found the word 'Lilliputian' and not 'Lilliputia' which meant small person or thing ,as in Gulliver's Travels and as her Mini was a small thing, Lilliputian seemed right.

The rain was lashing down, the wind was howling, it was dark and truly miserable. She reversed the Mini, and as she went through the gates she yelled out at the top of her lungs, 'WOOOOHOOO, my holiday has begun'. She turned the radio up and sang all the way home. 'Could it be you' by Cascada was playing, full blast.

The house was quiet when she arrived home from work. Her son was away at University and the cat and dog were in kennels. Her mum had taken them both there whilst Jasmine was at work as she couldn't face doing it herself. The Kennel was recommended by one of the Police Dog Handlers that Jasmine worked with. The kennels were individually heated, the dogs were all walked and played with every day and the kennel staff were true animal lovers. Her mum had left a note saying,

'Both Ruby and Bridget were fine, don't worry, have a wonderful holiday and see you soon. All my love Mum xxx'.

Her son, Alex, was studying art in Cardiff University. He was nineteen years old and had been living away for a year now. He came home during the holidays but mostly just slept and ate everything he could get his hands on when he did, but they had a good relationship and he had encouraged her to book a holiday. She had booked it for October as it was slightly cheaper than the rest of the year and besides, it was the only time she could book off as that was the only time available on her work rota. She had been on sick leave for her knee operation when the leave list went out to staff.

Jasmine was divorced from Alex's father, James, and had been on her own for seven years. They had been married for twelve years, mostly happy but not exceptionally. Later on in their marriage, James had started to drink heavily, started to come home from work later and later. He worked at a private company as a Safety Training Officer, teaching security to police and stewards on how to deal with all aspects of security breaches, unruly crowds and combat management. On one occasion, James had gone out to watch a rugby match at the local rugby club with his brother. Jasmine and Alex had gone on to bed early as Alex had school the next morning and Jasmine had work. James stumbled home in the early hours of the morning as drunk as a skunk. He was in a foul mood as the team he supported had lost the match. He marched up the stairs, flung the bedroom door open and yanked the duvet off Jasmine who had been sound asleep. She woke up with a start, saw what state he was in and tried to calm him down. This wound James up even more. He pushed Jasmine back on to the bed and fell on top of her. The stench of his alcohol fuelled breath made Jasmine feel ill. She tried to push him off her but he aggressively pushed his nose up against hers. He grabbed her throat with one hand, pushed her legs apart with his legs and with the other hand he forced himself into her. Jasmine struggled but the more she struggled the tighter his grip around her throat became. She couldn't breathe. Tears streamed down her face until finally he let go and fell off her in a drunken stupor. Once he had fallen asleep, Jasmine took herself off downstairs. She cried and cried and her whole body shook and rocked until the tears dried up.

He didn't attack her again like that. The drinking became heavier and he was never in any fit state to do anything physical. He verbally and mentally abused her every time he drank heavily, calling her fat and stupid and useless. Jasmine was too ashamed and lacked confidence by this time. She began to believe the sick things he would say about her and she had no self-worth. She was frightened of him. When he was sober he was as nice as pie to her but when he had been drinking he was pure evil. Jasmine would curl up in a tight ball, grip the edge of the bed until her fingers went white and numb every time she heard James stumbling up the stairs after a good drinking session.

She later discovered he had been sleeping with one of the women who worked in his office and she finally had the courage to throw him out. Jasmine's confidence had been shot. She hardly went out unless it was to work where it would take her mind off things. She hadn't told anyone she worked with. She was too ashamed. She stopped going out with friends, making excuses for not going here and there. She had her groceries, clothes and gift shopping delivered to her home. She would go to Alex's school for meetings and concerts but lingered at the back, out of sight. Her mum knew what had happened and visited her a lot. She had been a great support. Jasmine would even look and check out of the windows before taking the dog out as she didn't want to bump into the neighbours as she couldn't face talking to them. It took just over eighteen months before she started to feel like her old self again. The song, 'Because of You', by Kelly Clarkson, had become the anthem to her life at that time she thought.

She started to go out for the odd drink here and there with mates and slowly her confidence began to grow.

She had the odd fling, the odd Christmas party snog but nothing serious. She went on a date with an old school friend after she bumped into him in a pub one night whilst out with friends. He took her mobile number and rang her the next day for a date. He said he had a bike and would pick her up. Great thought

Jasmine, as she dugout an old leather jacket from the back of the wardrobe that she had hardly worn. The night he picked her up she was so excited. She wore skin tight jeans that showed off her curvy body. A tight black t-shirt type top and her leather jacket. The doorbell rang, she opened the door to find her date propping up a push bike against her wall. She laughed and said,

"C'mon, where's your motor bike?" After he shrugged his shoulders and said she could sit on the handle bars, and said he thought it would be a laugh, she slammed the door in his face and refused to answer his persistent door bell ringing and door knocker banging. What a plonker she thought but looking back he had been an idiot at school. Always the class jester, always being sent to the headmaster's office.

Another time she went out with a friend of friend and after a couple of dates they became quite intimate but after he had his wicked way with her, he told her he was going back to his wife from whom he had separated from six months previously. What a knob. She had tried internet dating but thought it was like shopping for men, and was really uncomfortable about it so she knocked it on the head, especially after she had been chatting on line on Uniform dating to a Naval officer, (supposedly,) who said he was based at RAF Culdrose in Cornwall, a place that held fond memories for Jasmine as she and her family used to holiday there ever year when she was a kid and they always went to the air shows at Culdrose, and loved it. She chatted to him for a few weeks and he decided it would be funny to constantly insult the Welsh, insult women and talk about the size of his willy! 'Ugh,' she thought.

Another time she chatted to a man who seemed okay to start with, looked pretty decent from his photos, talked fondly of his love for his job, which was train driver, loved his family, but all of a sudden turned into the devil when chatting one evening. He appeared to have been drinking heavily as several words were incorrectly spelled and then back to front such as he was ,'off pissed with worlllld'. Then from then on all he did was slag of his ex, telling her how much he hated her, and that revenge was a dessert best served cold.

She stopped all correspondence with him and disconnected herself from all dating sites that she was registered with after that. She felt as if she was too old, at forty three and a quarter, to be dating anyway.

'If that's all there was out there then I'll stay in a relationship with myself, my chocolate and my red, red wine' mused Jasmine.

Chapter 2

It was half past three in the morning and the alarm clock rang so loudly it was if it was anxious to wake up the entire world. Jasmine jumped out of bed, skipped around the bedroom in her thick fleecy pink pyjamas.

"Oh, I'm going to Hawaii, Oh across the Pacific sea", in the tune of, 'I'm going to Barbados', she sang out loud as she headed towards the bathroom.

She had packed her suitcase a week before, she just needed to add a few more bits and pieces, check that her passport, tickets, money and most importantly, her credit cards were in her handbag and she would be ready.

She had been using a coconut crème based shower gel for about two months as she had fallen in love with the little piece of writing it had on the front of the bottle, when she saw it in the supermarket.

It read,

'I'm going to a faraway place she said, just for a while….her toes wiggled in the warm sand and a silly seagull laughed and danced in the sweet wind'.

Jasmine knew the words off by heart and quoted it out loud every time she used it in the shower. Today she had meant it, she was going to a faraway land with warm sand……mmm, she thought.

Doors, windows were all locked, checked, double checked, triple checked, central heating set to come on low twice a day to stop the pipes freezing, lamp and radio plugged into a timer switch so they would come on for a couple of hours a night so it looked like someone was home, although her mum would pop in and check a couple of times for her. She was very security conscious after working in the police station for nine years and having to deal with victims of burglary and seeing how absolutely devastated they were on discovering that some 'shit' had been into their property.

'Right, let's go' she whispered to herself. She put her suitcase and bag in to the boot of 'Lickle Lilliputia'.

She was driving to the airport herself as it was too early in the morning to expect someone to take her and her flight back was a night flight as well, and it was only to Cardiff which was an hour away. It was the first time a flight to Los Angeles would be flying from Cardiff in a while, they had stopped flying from there several years ago. Then she would have a connecting flight to Honolulu airport, Oahu. Jasmine was glad she didn't have to drive to London, especially as the weather was still horrific. The rain was lashing down, leaves were blowing, branches were falling. Autumn had certainly arrived in style and this year it was colder than usual. Jasmine didn't care,

'Para-bloody-dise here I bloody come'!!!

Her flight was eight o'clock, it was now ten minutes past four, plenty of time thought Jasmine. She stopped off at the twenty four hour petrol station in Willow Vale, the village where she lived.

'Need to check the tyres, get petrol and some sweeties', she said to herself.

Jasmine pulled up right under the shelter of the garage as the rain had become torrential. She removed the dust caps on the tyres and checked them one by one then replaced them when the tyres were OK. She then drove to the petrol pump and filled up with petrol. Her long, just coloured, just trimmed, (two days ago), brunette hair was blowing in her face and she couldn't see how much she was putting in. It kept sticking to her the lip balm that she had generously applied on her lips to stop them becoming chapped. She brushed her hair away from her face and saw £25.26p on the pump. She was aiming to keep going to £26. It stopped on £26.01p.

Jasmine was annoyed and wondered why she could never stop dead on the amount she wanted. She always seemed to be one pence over.

'I bet the garages rig it,' she muttered to herself and frowned. Anyway, when all was done, she went into the petrol station shop, picked up some pear drops to suck on the plane to stop her ears from popping, and took them to the cashier to pay for them and the petrol. The cashier gave her a strange look but didn't say anything.

"Thanks" said Jasmine as the cashier handed her the receipt. Miserable cow, she thought. Onwards to the airport.

Chapter 3

Jasmine pulled into the car park at the airport after a quiet, stress free drive, other than the weather. She had already booked and paid for her space so all she had to do was show the parking attendant the ticket that she had printed off the internet, find her space and park up. She showed her ticket to a little Danny DeVito, lookey likey parking attendant who was sat inside his little booth. He had toast in one had and a mug of something hot in the other as the steam was steaming up his minuscule window and hatch. He waved her on and pointed straight ahead. There were quite a few cars there, some people just parking as well.

'16C, here we are ', she said to herself. Just as she was about to pull into her space, a little old lady was getting out of the passenger side of a Citroen C2 that was parked in the next space. She seemed to take forever. She had left the door open wide as she was putting her coat on, checking her handbag, checking the car, and checking her handbag again. Her husband had made his way around to the boot to get their suitcases out. Jasmine started to ease her way into her space but the old lady was stood in the way still, with the door open.

'Feck sake, come on', muttered Jasmine, but not moving her lips so the elderly lady didn't see her. Still the old lady was farting around, she took her coat off, checked the pockets then, with her back to Jasmine, proceeded to dig around in her backside for presumably what could only be to find her knickers. They had obviously disappeared up there as she was having a good old tug around. 'Ugh' winced Jasmine who was about to put her hand on the horn to get the old lady to move, when the husband shouted something and she jumped out of the way. She was struggling to put on her coat still as she slammed the car door, as the wind was so strong. Jasmine finally managed to park.

As she walked into the airport, there were quite a few queues building up. Her phone went off in her handbag. She took it out as she was walking towards the check in desk and there was a voice mail message from her friend Cerys. Cerys was also going with Jasmine to Hawaii but as usual she was running late.

"Lorry jack knifed on M4, running late, check in make sure you reserve my seat next to you. Meet you in bar with a large one in yer hand...Ha! See ya in a bit you sexy mutha."

Cerys was forty and beautiful. When she walked into a room men and women would stop what they were doing and just stare at her. She was five feet and nine inches tall, had a body to die for, even better than Elle MC - thingy, had long curly blonde hair, the brownest eyes and the cutest little freckles. Cerys was a police officer, a firearms officer and she was amazing at her job. She was very confident, loved the unknown of her day to day job, but most of all she was a people person. She knew how to get on the right side of people instead of causing conflict like a few of her male counterparts did. She also had a naughty streak as she could be loud, brash, down right slutty but always very funny.

Jasmine had met Cerys when she was based at the same police station several years ago. Jasmine didn't know at the time but Cerys preferred women to men and when they were out at a works party both of them were extremely drunk and Cerys attempted to kiss Jasmine, tongues and all. Jasmine, being polite and curious too, (as she had no luck with men she thought why not), sat there with lips slightly pursed then couldn't help but burst into laughter when their tongues started to entwine. Cerys did the same. She told Jasmine that she was gay and she had really fancied her so she thought she would try her luck, however, it didn't work, both said it felt like kissing a sister. Jasmine admitted that she had always wondered what it would be like to be with a woman, however she really, really liked men but was very flattered anyway.

Since that night they had been the closest of friends, sharing secrets, confiding in each other, gained advice from each other but fundamentally trusted each other one hundred percent. Neither had a friendship like it before, even with any of their partners they had in the past. Cerys was in a relationship with a woman called Steph, who was attractive although not stunning looking like Cerys, but they had an open relationship as Steph was an air hostess on long haul flights. They lived together but Steph wasn't home much and because of this they had both agreed to have flings with other women if they felt the need but as long as they came back together after wards. They had met at a nightclub in Swansea, dated for two months, and then Steph moved in with Cerys and they were still together six years later. The 'open relationship' thing worked for them perfectly.

Their flight was in two and a half hours so Jasmine thought she would check in then freshen up, then have a coffee before any alcohol passed her lips.

She was first in the queue to check in. The airport, 'checking in lady,' who had immaculate make up on, with flawless foundation and bright red lipstick, looked up from her desk and glared at Jasmine. Jasmine half smiled back and said,

"Hi, can I check in please?"

"Umm, yes", said the flight attendant, still glaring at Jasmine. Jasmine placed her suitcase on the conveyor belt, showed her passport to the check-in assistant.

"Would it be possible to have a seat by the window, preferably in the front row so no-one can lean their chair back into my lap and can I reserve a seat next to me for my friend who is running late, Cerys Roden is her name?" asked Jasmine.

The check in lady looked at the passenger list and confirmed Cerys was on the list.

She weighed and tagged Jasmine's suitcase, checked her passport again.

"Yes no problem" she said, then pointed Jasmine to the security check-in whilst she handed her a boarding pass, and also pointed in the direction of duty free and departure lounge area and said with a frown and a painted on smile.

"Have a nice holiday" but it was almost like a question. Strange thought Jasmine.

All checked in through security, Jasmine made her way to the nearest ladies loo to freshen up. She placed her handbag by the basin and looked in to the mirror.

"Oh my Gawd", she shouted out, "no wonder I kept getting strange looks". She had almost perfect black lines on her forehead, cheeks and chin, and black lines running under her eyes.

She looked like a cross between Alice Cooper and Adam Ant.

"How the hell" she said to herself, "bollocks, the dirt from the dust caps when I checked the tyres on my car at the garage".

Jasmine washed her face and applied fresh make up, brushed her hair, applied deodorant under her arm pits, then a dab of Coco Chanel on her wrists.

'Right, duty free shop and a coffee ', she thought.

"Let's get a magazine to browse whilst I have my coffee" she said to herself. "I'm talking to myself a lot" she also said with a grin whilst looking at her watch. "Hurry up Cerys".

As she was looking for a magazine, a woman was stood at the newspaper stand reading all the newspapers. This was one of Jasmine's pet hates, so as the woman, who was exceptionally skinny with a screwed up ferret type face, licked her thumb so she could freely flick over to the next page, Jasmine stood by the side of her and picked up a paper that was third below the top one. The woman saw Jasmine's glare, and slowly put the newspaper down, said something like,

"Is that the time", and slinked away.

Jasmine bought the paper as well, not that she really wanted it but she felt as if she was making a point.

As she sat down at a little table near the window she could see planes landing, and wondered why not many were taking off.

'Oh well let's have a look what the celebs have been up to', she thought as she opened her magazine. Her coffee was piping hot but smelt delicious and she couldn't wait to taste it. Her mobile phone started beeping. Messages from her mum, son and mates started to come through as they must have all just been getting up for work.

'Have a wonderful time, don't worry about the house. Let me know when you are there love Mum xx'

'Mam, party party party, you deserve it, bring me back some duty free booze' LOL ALEX xx'

'You lucky lucky bitch, Have a wicked time, wish I could be with you. Don't let 'C' lead you astray. Lots of Love Karen xx'

'We are coming next time, its p-ing down here.

Have fun and GET LAID for goodness sake, it's about time. Love you always'....Sarah and Griff xxx'

Jasmine chuckled and a stray snort came out as well. She coughed out loud to try and cover it up. A young couple asked if they could sit down at the table as all the others had started to fill up. She said yes, but kept a seat for Cerys.

The couple were really friendly and very over excited like two playful puppies that were about to wee on the carpet. They were both in the thirties and about to go on their honeymoon. They chatted constantly and finished each other's sentences. Mia, the woman, was very touchy feely, whilst Max, the bloke, was very animated. They were from Newport and had their wedding on the weekend before. They explained it had been very low key as they had wanted to have an extravagant honeymoon instead. They were also flying to LA, then flying onto Hawaii and they were also staying in the same hotel as Jasmine at The Turtle Bay Resort.

'What are the chances,' asked Jasmine. She also started to feel more excited as she and the couple were talking about their holiday. What a lovely, perfectly matched couple she thought.

They all shared stories and the laughter was getting louder. She felt a warm glow about her as she felt so lucky to be going to such a beautiful place.

Chapter 4

The weather had started to get worse and traffic controllers and baggage handlers had to run back under cover. The sky was black, the rain hammered down like there was no tomorrow, the wind howled and whirled any piece of debris it could gather. All the awaiting passengers had gathered by the windows. Someone shouted,

"It's snowing" then "What?" everyone yelled.

"It's only October", someone else squealed back as if that would make any difference.

Whoever alerted the now gathering crowd, including the airport shop staff, was right. It wasn't just snow, there were hail stones the size of rugby balls thundering from the sky, there were lightning bolts, and yet there was still rain. What the hell was going on?

A trembling voice over the tannoy announced,

"All flights, that's all flights have been cancelled for now due to the extreme and inclement weather conditions, please be patient and we will keep you updated, thank you."

A huge groan echoed around the departure lounge.

Jasmine checked her phone anxiously to see if Cerys had sent a message. There was no signal and no message.

'What if something has happened to her', she worried.

Everyone was making their way either to the food hall or to the bar including some of the airport staff. Jasmine made her way to the bar and Mia and Max, or 'M n M' as Jasmine decided to call them, followed her.

"I'll have a large vodka and diet coke please" said Jasmine when the bar tender asked what she would like.

"I will have the bloody same" shouted a familiar voice from behind her.

"Oh my gawd, are you okay?" Jasmine said as she hugged Cerys.

Cerys had arrived, checked in gone through security and had made her way straight to the bar with blood dripping from her knees.

"That bastard wind knocked me down so many times I ended up crawling into the main entrance of the airport dragging my suitcase behind me", Cerys said out loud and she downed her drink in one swoop.

"Another one please young bartender if you don't mind" she said as she waved her glass in the air.

"Sit down you crazy bitch, let me clean you up" said Jasmine as she took some wet wipes and tissues out of her bag.

"I parked my car near to 'Lickle fecking Lilliputia'" said Cerys angrily,

"And as I was walking to the airport entrance, the sky went black and, well you probably saw what happened. It was awful. People with kids and there were old people crawling and lugging their cases because they couldn't stand up in the wind and the rest of the shit that was coming from the sky. I expected a plague of locust to fly over as well. The worst thing was the little man in the car park booth had to run as the booth took off, it's probably half way across the Atlantic by now. We'll see it as we fly passed it when we finally get up in the air. I will be so glad to get away from the British weather."

Cerys rambled on like a mad woman, her experience had really shaken up her 'G I Jane' image.

"I'll tell you Jasmine, the devil is after me" she said solemnly as she squeezed Jasmine's forearm tightly.

"What, don't be daft", answered Jasmine, but Cerys held her stare for a while and looked away. It looked as though she was starting to well up but then changed her expression to a smile, the face that Jasmine was more familiar with.

Cerys and Jasmine went and sat down on a row of seats in the departure lounge. There were several small televisions on around the lounge and the news was reporting the unusual and bizarre weather conditions. The Met office reported that it was going to stick around for a few more hours then slowly drift off towards the North Sea and it was advisable that all flights, trains, buses, cars and all forms of transportation stopped until further notice.

"A few more hours?" said Jasmine, "Oh well, I suppose it's lucky we hadn't taken off and started flying in this storm, typical though, waiting all this time to go on my dream holiday and this happens".

She turned around from watching the television to see why Cerys hadn't chirped in but she was not there.

'Where has she gone now' wondered Jasmine as she frantically searched around the departure lounge with her eyes. She was reluctant to leave her seat as they were going to be there for a few hours and needed somewhere to be comfortable.

'She knows where I am so I'll stay here. Probably gone to the bar again or to the loo. Odd for her not to say though, unless I didn't hear her,' thought Jasmine.

She picked up her magazine that she had bought earlier and started to read it. After half an hour of who's seeing who, who is dumping who, which poor sod will be snared next by the famous plastic -titty model with numerous children by several different pop stars; who claims to have written loads of books but in reality she pays someone else to do it for her, Jasmine decided to read her book instead. She was reading a book written by Helen Fielding, and she was loving every page.

After another half an hour or so Cerys decided to return but only briefly after explaining where she had been and what she had been up to since.

Cerys told Jasmine she was going to the loo but Jasmine was too engrossed in the news and there was a lot of noise around them with upset passengers screaming at the airport staff, blaming them for the weather. There were kids running up and down the floor and then skidding on their knees to see how fast they could glide, so it's no wonder Jasmine didn't hear anything.

Cerys went on to explain how she had an erotic encounter with a gorgeous woman that she had met once before in a nightclub, in the loos!

"What" said Jasmine, "you dirty cow, what's the matter with you, and you're always on heat".

Cerys giggled. She went on to say she was washing her face, combing her hair and re applying her lipstick when she saw a woman in the mirror smiling back at her. Cerys said she turned around and they started chatting and she reminded her that they had met before and had spent a very eventful night together, but never saw each other or exchanged telephone numbers after that. The woman, called Louisa, said how beautiful

Cerys was and she was mesmerized by her. Cerys said how flattered she was and Louisa asked what perfume she was wearing as she reached for Cerys' wrist. Cerys said she was wearing Daisy by Marc Jacobs and with that Louisa sniffed her wrist. She stroked Cery's hair then cheek and reminded her what a hot time they had the last time they had met. The next thing they were snogging away in a loo cubicle and doing some very heavy petting.

Jasmine sat there with her mouth open, very tempted to ask more questions but she held her hand up to signal for Cerys to stop talking and waved her away.

"Go on you tart….I would say give her one for me but I'm not that way inclined" said Jasmine.

They both giggled and Cerys leaned over to kiss Jasmine on the cheek.

"I won't be too long" said Cerys.

"Don't worry, looks like we are going to here a while yet, I've got almost three more weeks of you anyway, so go and do whatever it is that you do...... and I'll look after your carry-on bag. I'll put it on your seat so no-one else can sit there".

Cerys blew Jasmine another kiss and mouthed the words,

'I love you', as she disappeared off into the noisy, restless, anxious group of passengers.

Again there was some commotion in the far corner with a group of passengers and airline staff. One of the staff, wearing a yellow high visibility waistcoat and carrying a radio, was trying to calm down a very large man and his very large wife. He was wearing a gawdy Hawaiian shirt and light blue chinos that were in fashion in the eighties and the wife had on what look like some sort of Kaftan. He was all red in the face saying he was going to miss the connecting flight from LA to Hawaii.

'I hope he isn't in our hotel' groaned Jasmine to herself.

The airline advisor was trying to explain that the flights were regular from LA and as soon as they knew what was happening themselves, they would arrange a connection flight for him and his wife and she emphasized loudly, that all the other passengers were in the same situation. She yelled back at him as he was trying to yell over the top of her whilst excreting a substantial amount of spit at the same time. She then took a deep breath and calmly told them to take a seat and be patient and walked away from him to answer other questions from other worried passengers.

In another part of the crowd, quiet a distance away, there was a group of very well dressed men, a little hard to see from where Jasmine was sitting but there was about six of them, all seemed quite good looking, ages ranging from early thirties to early forties. They were laughing out loud and jostling each other. Some were sitting and some were standing, when she could hear the odd word when they shouted at each other they sounded American. One of the men caught Jasmine's eye. She could make out he had light brown hair, good shaped body. He was wearing a black jacket and trousers and a dark shirt. She turned away so he wouldn't see her staring and after a minute or so she slowly turned back to see if he was still watching, he wasn't there.

'Hmmm, shame, oh well' she sighed.

That little episode with the angry passengers and the airline staff reminded Jasmine of her job, where sometimes she felt like she was hosting a show that involved people with poor social skills, bad manners and relationship issues. She gazed at the rude and over bearing passengers who were demanding unreasonable answers and unanswerable questions from the flummoxed airline staff.

Whilst thinking about the people she and her colleagues had to deal with at work, she recalled that, as regular as clockwork, in would walk two sisters amongst all the pandemonium, as they liked to get involved; who were both quite elderly; who dressed the same; neither of them have teeth, both have little, fluffy white beards and moustaches. They regularly popped into the station to see what was going on or to ask for any freebies that the police were giving away such as little bells to go on a purse which can be heard if someone attempts to steal it from a bag, or the little attack alarms that can go on key rings or stickers for a front door to stop cold callers ringing the doorbell.

They always asked for Jasmine's name and repeated it back several times to her. They would then post a card in the mail with numerous one pence stamps all over the front with the words,

' Jazzyminn thanks for help'. Quite sweet really.

Jasmine has about eighteen cards from them altogether from over the years and the other staff had the same if not more. They had been told loads of times not to waste their money but they wouldn't listen.

A few days before Jasmine started her holiday, she had a couple of funny incidents. She sat smiling to herself thinking about them. She wondered if the airport staff had strange and funny things happen to them.

One of them was a report from a male saying he was being stalked by a woman on the internet and by phone. She was constantly ringing him, leaving him naughty messages on his answer machine, sending him emails with nude pictures on and asking him for a good time. He had told her he didn't want to know but she still wouldn't leave him alone. When Jasmine questioned him a bit more she discovered he had met this woman on a sex internet site called 'F-buddy'. He had started chatting to her and sent her explicit photos by text of his naked and excited body. Jasmine really struggled to keep a straight face, not only because of the content on his complaint but he resembled Arthur Scargill with his comb-over hairstyle, he also had four chins and a pot belly and rancid breath to boot.

After really struggling to take this seriously she saw he was genuinely distressed by all of this and she gave him suitable advice on how to deal with his 'problem'. She told him to disconnect from the internet site and block her telephone number and email address so she couldn't contact him again.

Just before she closed the station up a few nights ago, she had a radio message from one of the officers, which had very poor radio reception asking her to contact the custody unit for him as he had a prisoner on board. She asked him what the offence was as the custody officer would probably ask, and all she thought she could hear from the arresting officer was,

'One coming in dressed to kill'.

She asked him to repeat it as it sounded odd, but it still sounded the same, so she rang the custody suite to inform them and the custody detention officer she spoke to thought it was hysterical. When the arresting officer arrived at the custody unit, he rang Jasmine in fits of laughter telling her that the offence was threats to kill, not dressed to kill! She blushed and laughed along with him.

She had also taken a call the same day from a woman who had been driving on the M4 motorway going towards the Severn Bridge saying she had to swerve as a lorry driver had lost all his load all over the carriageway. Jasmine contacted the traffic officers over the radio straightaway and told them that a lorry driver had shot his load over the carriageway. The radio went silent so she called him again and he tried to answer but couldn't contain himself. He was laughing so hard that he couldn't answer. She had phone calls from everyone who heard her message, all of them taking the mick! She mostly enjoyed her job but on occasion she felt as if she could just walk out when she was being abused or shouted at, only occasionally though.

Chapter 5

Jasmine, like loads of women, always dreamed of being whisked off by a gorgeous man dressed in a Naval Officers suit, like Richard Gere in the film, "An Officer and a Gentleman", to get away from sorting out the lives of some of the dysfunctional families in the front office at work. The man would be someone like the Canadian actor Leo McKenzie who played a Captain in the US army in the World War II television mini-series about the Pacific, based on real life soldiers, that she enjoyed so much. He epitomized the saying,

"Leaders should lead from the front and not from behind". He played the part with so much heart and soul and the reaction of the other Marines when he was shot by a Japanese sniper made Jasmine quiver all over. The real Captain, who was the commanding officer of King Company in the battle of the Pacific, was a true hero, as were all soldiers who went to any war, but he just stood out for Jasmine. The actor playing him would have done the real Captain so proud. She enjoyed the series so much she sent a message on Face book that was set up for the television mini-series, mentioning how exceptional she thought the actor had captured the role of the Captain. To Jasmine's astonishment, the actor, who played the role and whose name was Leo, replied to her and since then they sent each other quirky little messages, only general small talk, nothing major and she wasn't sure it was really him anyway.

When she was off from work on sick leave after her knee operation she watched loads of daytime TV mostly rubbish but got hooked on 'This Morning'. There were loads of stories from ordinary, everyday people and the presenters and producers more often than not had them on their show to talk to them, so Jasmine decided to write in about this amazing actor. He wasn't that well known in the UK but asked if it would be possible for the entertainment correspondent to interview him about a movie he was about to start filming. She wrote that he had told her on Face book about it when she asked about his up and coming projects. She went on to say he also told her that the WWII mini-series had just won several Emmy Awards. She asked if it would be possible for them to interview him and the cast and it would also be the seventy year anniversary in December that year, 2011, of the attack on Pearl Harbour.

She didn't hear anything from Holly and Phil the presenters or the producers, so she wrote to Alison Hammond, the Big Brother contestant who was extremely lucky to get a job as a presenter on 'This Morning'. Again, she didn't hear anything, although she got a signed photo of Holly and Phil!

Anyway, in her fantasy, this hero would carry her out of the police station, kissing her as they walked away out into the back yard, she would stick her middle finger up to her boss as he gawped at her out of his office window, yelling at her to get back to work or else and colleagues would shout out after her,

"Way to go Jasmine, way to go".

They would ride off on his motorbike into the sunset...aw!

She wished and dreamed but in reality she was just really glad to be going on holiday away from the daily grind.

There is nothing wrong with dreaming...right?

Chapter 6

Jasmine suddenly jumped, she must have dozed off when she was reading her book. There was no sign of Cerys, she must be having a good time thought Jasmine. She rubbed her eyes and sat up straight. It was still dark outside from the storm clouds but the terrifying wind and hail storm seemed to have eased off, but it was still raining heavily.

There was still no movement of airline staff out on the runway and none of the planes had taken off.

Jasmine yawned and stretched out her arms. She dropped her book and her homemade book marker fell out. She picked up her book but couldn't see where the book marker was. It was a silly book marker made up of pictures of her favourite male singers and movie stars, such as Hugh Jackman, Richard Gere, Will Smith, Jon Bon Jovi and of course the latest edition, the actor Leo McKenzie aka the Captain. A bit childish she had thought when she was putting it together but hey... who cares, it was hers and it was nice to look at.

As she bent down on her knees to search under the chairs opposite to her she found a Canadian penny. She picked it up and said to herself,

'Find a penny pick it up and all through the day you'll have good luck'.

"Pin" someone said behind her, she stood up to see an old man sitting in her seat.

"What?" she asked

"It's find a pin and pick it up" said the old man. He had a deep North American accent, his mouth muffled by a huge, bushy moustache. He had thick white eyebrows and a ruddy complexion. He didn't have the shape of an old man although he was slightly hunched forward. He had what looked like safari clothes on, khaki shirt that was tucked into his khaki trousers with the waist band almost around his chest.

"Oh right" replied Jasmine, "I was always taught it was a penny not a pin. Different cultures I s'pose" she said. The man looked familiar thought Jasmine.

"Is it your penny, are you Canadian?" she asked.

He muttered something under his moustache, took the penny from her hand then showed her that he had found her book marker. Before he handed it over to her he examined the pictures on it. Jasmine blushed.

"Daft I know, but it keeps me smiling" she said as he handed it to her. He smiled back, almost grinning. He gave her back the penny.

"It's a gift", he said.

"Why are you giving me a gift?" quizzed Jasmine.

He held her stare for a few seconds then waved as he stood up,

"It just is", he mumbled and shuffled his way off into the crowd.

"Thank you Mr um Mr whoever you are". How odd she thought. 'Daft ol' bugger', she muttered under her breath.

Before sitting back down she had a good look around to see if she could see Cerys. No, still no sign. She looked at the penny again, and put it in her pocket.

'Maybe it will bring me luck, I'll make a wish and throw it into a fountain or something when I get to Hawaii', she told herself.

As she sat down she heard a group of people singing. She stood up again to see where the voices were coming from. She stood on her seat and saw a band near to the sweet stand. They were playing guitars, keyboard and beating a drum. They started to belt out Bon Jovi songs, now, Jasmine adored Bon Jovi. She had seen them in 2008 in Bristol, when she went with Cerys, her partner Steph, and their friends Mark, Julie and Gethin. They had managed to push their way to the front and stand right underneath Richie Sambora, the greatest guitar player in the world thought Jasmine.

One of the best concerts she had ever been to in her life.

Before long the majority of the passengers were clapping and raising their hands in the air to 'Livin on a prayer'. The atmosphere was incredible. Jasmine scanned the room for Cerys, she saw her at last. What was she doing talking and laughing with the group of well-dressed and groomed men she saw earlier? Jasmine tried to catch her eye by jumping up and down, but everyone was doing the same as they were rocking to the Bon Jovi tribute band. Cerys finally turned around and so did the man she saw watching her earlier. Cerys waved to her, turned back, threw her head back in laughter and waved at them all as she walked away and towards Jasmine.

"Where have you been Cerys, and who are those men?"

Jasmine climbed off her chair and sat down, Cerys sat down next to her.

"Well I have been having a bit of fun with Louisa, and we sort of couldn't stop when we got outside of the ladies loo, you know what I mean?"

"Aw c'mon Cerys I am pretty open minded but you are disgusting" said Jasmine.

"I know, sorry, but she was so hot, I couldn't stop, she was like a drug. Anyway, those guys over there" she pointed to the men she had been talking with.

"They saw us and gave a round of applause. Obviously we stopped, and we felt a little embarrassed that we got caught. I got her number anyway. She is travelling with a group of friends and family to a wedding in LA so if it's okay with you, I will meet up with her in LA."

Jasmine tutted, "yeah okay" she said.

They had a night stopover in LA before getting their connecting flight the next day to Oahu.

Cerys had planned to have dinner with Louisa and Jasmine before spending the rest of the night with Louisa. Jasmine agreed to this. She was planning on going to bed early anyway as they had to be up at five o'clock the next day to go back to the airport.

"Hey, also Jazzy baby", said Cerys is a Betty Boop type voice,

"One of the guys that caught me and Louisa locking lips in public was asking about you. He is really cute. He is flying to LA, lives there and works there sometimes apparently. He and the other blokes have been here for a meeting or something. I wasn't really taking much in, as I was coming down from euphoria" she giggled.

"Oh, he asked who I was travelling with, and where we were going. I pointed over to you and I'm sure he said you looked nice. He said you were pretty and asked if you were into men or women so I made sure he knew you definitely liked men".

"Cerys, for goodness sake, what are you my pimp or something?"

Cerys laughed.

"I told him your name and where we were staying so watch this space", she winked.

Jasmine glanced across the departure lounge but she couldn't see 'her admirer'.

Cerys and Jasmine made their way to the bar for a top up.

Finally, the dark sky lifted and the clouds became lighter and the rain eased. There was movement outside on the runway. A group of passengers who were seated by the windows gave a cheer which alerted everyone else. A tannoy message filled the air.

"Attention please, the weather has eased and the flight LX 472D from gate 22 to LAX Los Angeles will be boarding shortly. Please can the first class passengers start to make their way to gate 22, first class passengers to Los Angeles to gate 22 please. Please listen out for Premier class and then economy. Thank you and thank you for your patience."

The mood lifted and people started to gather their belongings. The first class passengers cockily moved off to get on the plane first, no doubt to get their champagne and a foot massage before the 'poor people' got on to lower the tone.

Finally Jasmine and Cerys were settled in their seats on the plane. They had two seats together with no-one sat next to them and at the front of the row with no-one sat in front of them. Jasmine opted for the window seat on the out flight and Cerys had the picked the window seat coming back, forgetting that it was a night flight coming home.

'Tidy', said Cerys.

The take-off was smooth and once up in the air, out came the air stewards with drinks and nibbles. Cerys stood up to put her carry-on bag in the overhead luggage compartment after she had sorted out what she wanted to put in her handbag. She had taken out a clean pair of knickers which read,

'All you can eat buffet' written on the front; roll on deodorant and a book. She had given Jasmine a pair of knickers as part of her birthday present and on the front it said,

'I would do anything for love' and on the back it said,

'But I won't do that'. Jasmine had packed them in her bag just in case she had the opportunity to wear them. As Cerys reached up to shut the door of the overhead compartment her low cut top popped down revealing her very shapely and ample cleavage. The teenage brothers in the seats behind giggled out loud. Their parents were sat behind them, tutting and poking their sons to stop laughing.

"Sorry lads, you have now met my friends flip and flop", Cerys said brazenly.

Jasmine grabbed Cery's arm and pulled her down into her seat as Cerys covered herself up.

'Behave" scowled Jasmine, but they both collapsed with laughter.

"Sorry, it was an accident", said Cerys.

The girls sat their chatting away and drinking their complimentary wine. They were so excited about their holiday.

They listened quietly to an interesting but sick conversation going on between the two brothers sat behind them. One was about sixteen years old and the other about fifteen years old. They were talking about different kinds of poops!

The oldest one said,

" The mystery shit is the best because you struggle to push it out, it plops really loudly then when you look it's gone and when you wipe your butt, there ain't nothing there to wipe, it's awesome."

The younger brother chipped in.

"Yeah and then there's the secret explosion, that's when you plop out a tiny rabbit pellet and then you wipe your butt and you have to use half a toilet roll as it's so messy".

They both went quiet as if sitting their contemplating what each other had just said.

Jasmine and Cery's looked at each other quietly grimacing and mouthing 'ugh' to each other.

They both settled down to watch some in-flight entertainment. Cerys watched the new 'Planet of the apes' film whilst Jasmine watched old comedy shows. She watched 'The Dave Allen show'. He was an Irish comedian she used to watch when she was a child with her mother and brother. She watched the one with Dave Allen explaining to the audience how he taught his child to tell the time. It was hysterical when he was saying there are three hands on the clock, the first is the hour hand, the second is the minute hand and the third is the second hand and the child didn't get why the third hand was called the second hand. Jasmine had tears rolling down her cheeks with laughter.

After a couple of hours into the ten and a half hour flight, the stewards served a meal of chicken or beef, with green beans, boiled potatoes, bread roll and dessert which was cheesecake followed by cheese and biscuits. The steward served Jasmine and Cerys but gave them real glass champagne flutes. Everyone else were given plastic 'glasses'.

Then another steward appeared from behind the curtains with a white cloth over her arm and a large, what appeared to be, magnum of champagne, that had already been corked, and started pouring it into Jasmine and Cery's glasses.

"Um, what, I mean why", said Cerys in a surprised, helium-type inhaled voice but the steward snootily interrupted and said,
"It's a gift from one of the other passengers who wishes to remain anonymous. I will be back to refill your glasses later". With that she turned and wiggled off and disappeared behind the 'secret' curtain that divided the galley and different class of passengers.

"Oooh, lush" said Jasmine as she took a sip of her champagne that fizzled and bubbled under her nose.

"Has to be from Louisa, can't wait to get a piece of this sex on legs", said Cerys coquettishly.

Jasmine frowned at her for a second, but then thought, oh well, she was happy to drink the bubbly as long as she didn't have to do anything in return as a thank you. Cerys would do that for her.

After another refill and several trips to the loo, Cerys and Jasmine watched a bit more in flight television and dozed on an off until they finally reached Los Angeles.

They stepped off the plane, and the heat hit them immediately. The sun was beating down, the sky was an orangey, yellowy glow and the air smelt sweet.

Chapter 7

It was two thirty in the afternoon there, but back in Wales, UK, it was ten thirty in the night. It felt strange but both Jasmine and Cerys were bouncing with tired excitement.

After the rigorous security checks, immigration and luggage collection the exhausted travellers made their way on foot, dragging their suitcases behind them, with way too many clothes, and shoes inside, to the hotel which was literally located at the entrance to the airport.

Once checked in they went to their separate rooms to freshen up and to contact family to say they had arrived in LA. They had arranged to meet in an hour to go and explore during the very few hours they had there and Cerys was meeting up with her friend Louisa later so they needed to find a restaurant nearby so she could call her and arrange for her to meet her and Cerys there later.

Jasmine went into her room which was next door to Cerys'. They decided to have separate rooms because they would keep each other up all night giggling and chatting and playing pranks on each other like school girls on a camping holiday and it always happened when they shared a room previously, besides, Cerys normally 'pulled' and poor Jasmine had to wait in the bar until it was ' all clear'.

Jasmine's room was luxurious, not like some of the dumps she had stayed in the UK.

The bed was queen sized with a crisp white and gold duvet cover and matching pillows and curtains, the T.V was also 'queen sized', and the bathroom had granite counter tops and marble tile floors.

There was free Wi-Fi, a hairdryer, and a coffee maker.

Jasmine popped the coffee maker on and spread out across the bed…..'Mmmm'…..she said to herself.

After a coffee, a shower and fresh change of clothes, bit of lippy and blusher, she felt as new and fresh as a spring daisy. She put on a pale blue, sleeveless, low back maxi dress that covered any lumps and bumps that she thought she had, which she didn't, but showed off her toned arms and curvy shape. She was five feet and five inches tall and had really struggled with her weight over the years. Since booking her holiday to Hawaii she had completely changed her shape, by eating healthily and running every day. She was now more toned and almost confident with her shape. The dress wasn't too long or too short but felt just right. She slipped her dainty feet into her white, backless, spool heeled sandals that she had bought in a sale in the local 'Next' store about three years ago for fifteen pounds but had never had an occasion to wear them. She had worn them around the house to mould them in and make them comfortable a couple of times, but never out anywhere. She put her flowery, flat, toe post sandals in her bag as a backup. She added a small pale blue flower hair clip to her hair and pinned it in just behind her ear. It complimented her blue eyes and her olive skin. Her shiny, brunette, wavy hair was down over her shoulders. She had read in a magazine that LA women were all size zero and she didn't want to stand out and look like a human-hippo.

She sent texts to her mum and son to say she was in LA as she didn't want to ring them due to the time difference even though they probably wouldn't have minded, and no doubt Alex was out partying somewhere like students seemed to do all night and every night.

Cerys knocked on the door and shouted,

"C'mon Jas, let's see what this town has got to offer us sexy Welsh babes".

Jasmine opened the door, Cerys was wearing tight white three quarter length trousers, and a light pink short, low cut, short sleeved blouse that displayed her very well proportioned cleavage. She had matching light pink wedged sandals on. Her long blonde hair was put up into a loose bun. She looked like a super model and Jasmine felt a teensy bit jealous. Yet, Cerys thought Jasmine looked as equally gorgeous.

"I rang Louisa and she suggested she meets us here at the hotel at eight o'clock, as she says her cousin, who is getting married in LA, told her it was great food and overall really pleasant, plus she would get dropped off here by her cousin and get picked up in the morning, if you know what I mean". She winked.

"That's fine with me, right let's go and speak with reception to find out where we can go for a couple of hours then" said Jasmine jauntily.

The girls didn't have much time in LA because of the flight delay back home and the early flight the next morning so the hotel receptionist, who was very petite, typical Californian, with a beautiful bronze tan and perfect teeth suggested a bit of retail therapy at Westfield Culver City where they could find stores like Macy's and JC Penneys. They went via shuttle bus that only took twenty minutes. This was an adventure in itself as obviously the Americans drove on the 'wrong side' of the road, well, to Jasmine and Cerys they did.

After two hours Jasmine and Cerys decided to head back to the hotel, freshen up again and make their way to the restaurant to meet Louisa.

They hadn't bought much at the shopping centre other than a tacky, 'I heart LA' t-shirt that Jasmine had bought for Alex, and a new pair of aviator sunglasses as Cerys had broken the lens on her pair back in Cardiff when she fell over in the gale force wind outside the airport.

Back at the hotel Cerys and Jasmine made their way to the restaurant to meet Louisa. They were escorted to a table by a very smiley waiter who kept repeating 'you're welcome' every time either Jasmine or Cerys said thank you.

Louisa arrived just as the girls were ordering a bottle of wine.

"Hiya ladies", said Louisa. "How are you liking L.A?"

Cerys stood up and kissed her on the cheek, she seemed very excited, like a little girl who was about to get a new toy.

"Well, we haven't seen much, just a bit of shopping, we will have to come here again and stay longer, not just have a stopover. How about you?"

As Louisa sat down she gave a little wave to Jasmine, she went on to say,

'Oh my Gawd, my cousin's house is beautiful, just like you see on Beverly Hills 90210. It has a swimming pool and everything', she gushed. Louisa was twenty nine and a receptionist at a large gymnasium and leisure complex in Swansea, She was just as ordinary as Jasmine and Cerys and not used to the extravagance and way of life the Americans seemed to have. Everything was bigger, there seemed to be more optimism and hope there. Probably due to the abundance of sunshine, in LA anyway, which always brought the best out of people.

Her aunt, uncle and cousin moved to LA four years previously as her uncle was part of a large I.T company that had set up an office in Los Angeles and they offered him a job there. Her cousin, Sara, was eighteen when they moved and she had trained as a beautician along with Lousia's aunt Brenda and they both worked in the same salon. Sara had met her husband to be, Jared, who was six years older than her, whilst working at the beauty salon. He had popped in on the off chance to get his haircut as his regular barber shop was shut due to the owner having a stroke.

Jared was a school teacher and asked Sara out on a date as he said that he liked her accent. Two years later they were getting married and had invited Louisa and her parents to the wedding. Louisa's parents had arrived several days before her as they had taken a trip to Las Vegas first.

Jasmine ordered a sea food platter, Cerys had grilled chicken and salad and Louisa, typical young Brit, ordered burger and fries.

'Oh, by the way', chirped Cerys and she took a sip of chardonnay,

'Thank you for the Champers on the plane, it was lush'.

'Are you taking the mick?' asked Louisa. 'What are you talking about?' she asked as she took a bite out of her flame grilled burger.

'We were given a bottle of champagne on the plane, a gift from another passenger on the plane, c'mon, of course it was you, wasn't it?' questioned Cerys.

'Nope, not me' said Louisa.

'How odd. I bet they gave it to the wrong passengers…ooops' laughed Jasmine.

They chatted and laughed for ages. Jasmine started to yawn.

'I'm really sorry girls but I am knackered, it's been a long day, so do you mind if I head on up to bed?' she asked.

'See you bright and early' winked Cerys.

'Goodnight, lovely to meet you Louisa, hope the wedding goes well and I hope, maybe to see you again sometime', said Jasmine.

Louisa giggled and mumbled something back, she was a little tipsy and obviously had other things on her mind.

Jasmine paid the bill and left a tip and headed off to her room, still wondering about the champagne on the plane. She felt a bit guilty as it was obviously meant for someone else.

Cerys and Louisa sneaked off to Cerys' room. They couldn't keep their hands off each other in the elevator. It was lucky that no-one else was in there with them otherwise they could have been arrested.

'You are so fucking sexy' said Cerys as she pressed herself up against Louisa. They were so engrossed and embedded in each other's lips they hadn't realised the elevator door had opened when they had arrived at their floor.

As the door opened two men got in, grinning from ear to ear as they had seen two women kissing and groping each other.

'Am I dreaming?' said one of the men.

Cerys and Louisa adjusted themselves and Cerys took hold of Louisa's hand and fled out of the elevator, laughing as they ran.

'Sorry guys you are just not our type', Louisa called back.

Cerys looked back. She was sure she had seen those blokes at Cardiff airport but soon turned to her attention to Louisa who whispered,

'I'm so very very wet'.

The hotel room closed behind them as they both groaned with pleasure as they climbed into bed together.

Jasmine was in her room cleaning her teeth when she noticed, whilst looking in the bathroom mirror, that there was a single coral coloured, bell shaped flower on her pillow. She went into the bedroom, biting her toothbrush between her front teeth and hesitantly picked up the flower whilst looking around the room. After reassuring herself that no-one else was there and that the door was locked, she picked up the flower. The fragrance was so sweet, so fresh.

'Of course' she thought. 'This is California, they don't put little chocolates on the pillow here as they don't eat carbs, hence the flower, how beautiful is that'. She smiled to herself.

She gently smelt the flower again before placing it in a little glass of water by her bed.

The alarm clock woke Jasmine up from a deep sleep. She awoke to the glorious fragrance of the little flower and remembered that she was off to Hawaii that day....HAWAII...yippee.

Jasmine met Cerys in the hotel lobby. She had put the little flower in her button hole in her blouse. Louisa had already left as her cousin had picked her up on her way to the gym. The people of Los Angeles were obsessed with working out Louisa had told Cerys. The folk of LA went to bed early and woke early the following morning apparently.

Cerys gave Jasmine a hug.

"Here we go Jas. Let's go to Paradise. Mind you, I went to paradise last night. I had a wonderful time, Louisa was bloody fantastic, I'm still tingling! I am on a mission to find you a bloke when we get to Oahu".

"Cerys, for fuck sake, get your mind out of the gutter for once, we are not in Magaluf. I am not looking for a bloke, I just want to have a holiday of a lifetime with my best mate, now c'mon".

"Sorry", said Cerys, "I should have been born a man. Just love women and sex.... sorry babe. Pretty flower by the way".

The girls got on the shuttle bus that took them to LAX to catch their connecting flight to Oahu.

Chapter 8

After a five hour flight to Oahu the plane came to a standstill at Honolulu airport.

The passengers disembarked and made their way into the airport to be met by Hawaiian greeters. There were two women, both dressed in purple and white uniforms, hair tied tightly back off their faces, giving the traditional Oahu Lei, a single strand of flowers that is worn like a necklace, to passengers that wanted them. It was so exciting. One or two of the passengers, who had had enough of waiting around airports and travelling endlessly waved off the greeters as they tried to hand them a Lei. The rest of the passengers were happily accepting them.

Everyone made their way to the Wiki Wiki bus which took them to the baggage area.

Jasmine and Cerys collected their suitcases and after the rigorous security checks yet again, they searched through the crowd for their welcome signs with their names on. They had booked a taxi to take them to their hotel. They eventually saw a very large man with the biggest bald head they had ever seen holding a sign that said ' Jazzmin Williams and Kerris Roaden'. He looked like a giant baby.

"Come on Jazzy" laughed Cerys, "Our carriage awaits".

"Aloha. Welcome to Hawaii," said the driver as he loaded the boot, or trunk as they call it, with Jasmine and Cerys' luggage.

The sky was the bluest of blue, the sun was glowing and there was a warm gentle breeze. The air smelt fragrant and salty.

"You from England, I love tha' English accent" said the driver, who was called 'Lolly' and was a South Pacific native he told the girls. He was huge and almost filled the front of the taxi.

"Well, not England, Wales, which is a country in Britain" answered Jasmine. It always annoyed her that people from other countries thought that Britain only consisted of England, not that she had anything against England.

The driver just nodded as if he knew what she meant but clearly he didn't.

They drove along a coast road and they could see the huge monstrous waves beating against the glorious, rugged, luscious, coastline. It was absolutely beautiful, even better than the scenes from 'Hawaii Five-O' and 'Lost'.

As the taxi pulled up to the front of the resort, Jasmine clutched Cery's hand. They had never seen anything like it. They had spent almost every last penny of their savings on this holiday and they had been saving for a while, Jasmine more than Cerys as her wages were a lot less. It was a once in a lifetime holiday, so they went all out. Jasmine had tears rolling down her cheeks. She was crying with joy as she was thinking how lucky she was; a valley girl in Hawaii seemed unreal. Her dream had come true.

The hotel had picturesque views of the Pacific Ocean from every guest room and had a unique oceanfront location on the North shore of Oahu.

The hotel receptionist was checking in the couple, Mia and Max, that Jasmine had met at Cardiff airport. They were so excited and all Jasmine and Cerys could hear was,

"Oh my Gawd, oh my Gawd, oh my Gawd". The receptionist congratulated them on their wedding and she rang for a bell boy to take their luggage and show them to their suite.

"Oh hiya" said Mia. "Isn't this gorgeous? See you around". Mia and Max gazed into each other's eyes as they followed the bellboy.

"I'll give it two years" whispered Cerys.

"Aloha, my name is Marla" said the receptionist.

"Aloha" said Jasmine and Cerys at the same time, and then giggled... at the same time.

"We are Jasmine Williams and Cerys Roden, checking in please".

"Are you on honeymoon too?" smiled the receptionist.

"Umm, no, we are just friends, nothing like that", muttered Jasmine.

"I have tried to convert her, but no luck," laughed Cerys

The receptionist laughed as well.

"Well, George will take your luggage and show you to your room. It is a two bedroom suite so you can each have your privacy in the night and then join each other in the day. There are several restaurants, bars and grills in the resort when you are hungry, you can also ring for room service if required. There are menus in your room. There are quite a few trips that we can organise for you if you want us to. Again, all the information is in a welcome pack in your room. Please ring reception anytime day or night if you need anything. Enjoy your stay here at the Turtle Bay Resort".

The room was….well there were no words to describe it. It was an 'Ilima' Suite which overlooked the Ocean and the Turtle Bay Resort. It was a palatial suite featuring a wet bar, living room table and chairs, a sofa and had two connecting bedrooms. Each room had a king size bed. The bathroom had a full size roll top bath, and a shower. There was also a large private lanai, which is an open roofed porch or veranda, it was like another room.

Jasmine and Cerys stood in the middle of the suite absolutely gob smacked. George hung around, politely smiling and nodding his head, probably thinking how the hell these two hicks can afford this and wondering about his tip.

Both the girls gave him a ten dollar tip each. He seemed to be happy with that. Neither really understood the tipping system in the USA, even in LA they think they 'over tipped.' They were going to run out of money if they didn't find out how much they should tip.

The sound of the ocean could be heard all around the resort. It had almost five miles of beachfront and the ocean front resort setting immersed the guests in the natural tranquillity of the North Shore but was only forty five minutes from the energetic pulse of Honolulu and Waikiki City.

"This is stunning", said Jasmine as she quickly unpacked and put on her bikini and sarong. She sat on the veranda or the 'lanai'.

"I am so happy Cerys".

"Me too and I couldn't imagine coming here with anyone else except you Jas, not even Steph. I love you mate, you know that right?" asked Cerys as they two of them hugged and then took in the heavenly view of the resort.

The time was eleven hours behind that in Britain so rather than ring home, Jasmine sent a text to her mum and Alex.

'Arrived in paradise, absolutely beautiful, miss you both, will ring you in a few days when I've got my bearings. Love you both lots and lots xxx'.

Cerys did the same. She sent a message to her partner Steph and also her dad.

The next few days they spent exploring, relaxing and organising trips. They had organised a trip to Pearl Harbour and the USS Arizona Memorial, a Wild Side Specialty Tour, which was a whale watching, dolphin and turtle watching experience. They also booked an evening of entertainment and great food at the hotel's very own beach Luau.

Pearl Harbour was the first trip they decided to go on, it was something they had planned on doing for a while. It was something they had to do, something everyone should do like visiting Ground Zero in New York or the memorial sites for the Holocaust Victims, any memorial sites that were places that history took a turn and changed all of our lives, everyone's lives really, forever.

The weather was beautiful, although a little humid. Jasmine was having a really bad hair day because of the humidity so decided to scoop her brunette frizzy mass, which was normally shiny and wavy, up on top of her head into a knot. Not many people could carry this look off but it did rather suit her. She wore a sleeveless dark purple dress that came to just above the knee and cream low heeled wedged shoes. She took along an oversized bag to carry her camera, sunscreen, sunglasses and a change of shoes, just in case her feet hurt.

Cerys wore a strappy and very colourful knee length dress with white gladiator sandals. Her beautiful blonde hair was scooped up into a cheerleader type ponytail. You could imagine her grabbing some pom poms and shouting, "give me a wooo-hoo".

They took a bus trip to Pearl Harbour. It was lovely and cool as the air conditioning blasted out, the sound of the local radio station was playing in the background and the DJ was announcing the next song, a medley of Israel K's greatest songs. The rhythmic sound of the ukulele started to play and the sweetest voice started to sing.

"Want a chewing gum?" asked Cerys as she held out a packet of Orbit to Jasmine. "No thanks love, I am really excited and nervous about this trip, you know what I mean?" replied Jasmine.

"Yeah, it's gonna be intense" said Cerys. They both sat quietly all the way there as a tour guide, who was a little old chap, must have been in his late 80s early 90's, and was wearing khaki trousers and a matching shirt and a matching baseball cap, gave a little talk about Pearl Harbour. Firstly he played a recording of an announcement.

"Yesterday, December 7th 1941, a date which will live in infamy, the United States of America was suddenly and deliberately attacked by naval and air forces of the Empire of Japan".

The tour guide, who was called Tom, went on to say that was an announcement by the President of that time,

Franklin Delano Roosevelt. There was a sudden hush amongst everyone on the bus.

As they arrived at Pearl Harbour the group of people that were on the same bus as Jasmine and Cerys all grouped together as Tom the tour guide, still carrying his microphone, gathered everyone together. He started talking and waving at everyone and pointing at the memorial site for USS Arizona.

"Pearl Harbour, named for the pearl oysters once harvested there, is the largest natural harbour in Hawaii, a World War II Valour in the Pacific National Monument and the only naval base in the United States to be designated a National Historical Landmark. The devastating attack on Pearl Harbour resulted in two thousand, three hundred and ninety dead and hundreds wounded, and drove the United States into World War II. Pearl Harbour honours this history changing event with the Pearl Harbour Historic Sites".

At the visitor centre the group watched a short film about the attack and then viewed plaques honouring lives lost on that fateful day.

Tom then ushered everyone in his group towards a shuttle boat. As everyone was climbing on an elderly English couple who were at the back of the group began yelling at each other.

"For goodness sake, shut up Fred, this happened seventy years ago, stop going on about it", said the very petite, very well spoken lady, who had the whitest hair.

"Bloody Yanks, didn't want to join in the war until this happened, yeah you heard" he turned around and waved his walking stick at everyone. He stormed off in his oversized beige shorts, blue shirt, open toe sandals with black socks, and his brown flat cap, and made his way back towards the bus.

"Bloody Yanks", he shouted again.

His wife, who looked very embarrassed tried to shout out,

"So sorry" to everyone, but it came out in a whisper. She looked back at her husband, who was shouting at another bus load of tourists who had just turned up.

"Okay to carry on ma'am?" asked Tom the tour guide.

"Yes, yes of course", she croaked, "so sorry".

"Don't worry ma'am, come right up front with me and you can have the best views if you so wish or would you like to return to the coach with the gentleman?"

The lady brushed down the front of her skirt, lifted her shoulders and walked up to Tom and linked her arm into his.

Everyone quietly chuckled to themselves.

"You go granny", muttered Cerys under her breath and Jasmine nodded in agreement.

As they all arrived at the USS Arizona Memorial, Tom began speaking into his microphone again.

"Everyone ok?"

"Yes", said everyone in harmony.

Cerys suddenly grabbed her stomach.

"Ooooh" she said in pain

"You OK Missy?" said Tom and everyone turned and looked at Cerys

"Yes, I'm fine, too much of the Hawaiian Rum punch I think," she grumbled.

Everyone turned to face Tom again.

"What's up Cerys, are you OK?"

"Aw I'm fine, probably period pains".

Jasmine could see something wasn't right with Cerys. She had never complained of period pains before and if Jasmine ever complained about her period pains Cerys would call her a wimp and a wuss. She held her arm as they continued with their tour. Cerys tried to put on a smile for Jasmine but she could see it was forced.

Tom began again.

"At 8.06 am on December 7th 1941, the USS Arizona was hit by a 1760 pound armour piercing bomb, which ignited its forward ammunition magazine. The catastrophic explosion that resulted sank this massive battleship in nine minutes, killing 1177 crewmen."

There was a loud gasp from the group, Cerys' arm tightened around Jasmine's.

Tom continued.

"Today, the USS Arizona Memorial is a place to learn about the historic attack and pay your respects to the brave soldiers that fell that day. Take a look around you folks."

Slowly Cerys and Jasmine looked around the memorial site.

"Phew, feeling better now, sorry about that, don't know what came over me…daft cow aren't I?" said Cerys, straightening herself up and letting go of Jasmine's arm.

"Are you sure you are OK?" asked Jasmine as she squinted not really believing her.

"Yes, c'mon", smiled Cerys convincingly.

Tom came over the microphone again.

"The USS Arizona is a floating memorial built over the sunken hull of the Battleship USS Arizona, the final resting place of the ship's crew. In the shrine room a marble wall exhibit's the names of the men who lost their lives on the Arizona. Poignant and powerful, this is a place where visitors come face to face with the devastating effects of war."

After the tour, everyone in the group felt quite sombre. Everyone was quiet, as if they were in deep thought or even prayer.

Jasmine felt quite saddened by it all. She hugged Cerys as they were walking back to the shuttle.

Cerys who seemed to be back to her old self playfully yelled, "Get off you are not my type", but put her arms around Jasmine anyway.

As they were waiting for the boat shuttle to take them back, Jasmine started talking to other members of the group about the tour whilst Cerys moved over to talk to a group that had followed theirs. They had another tour guide called Morris who was having a quick chat to Tom.

"Hiya", shouted Cerys as she disappeared amongst a group of tourists. Jasmine turned around to see who she was greeting, was it someone she knew? Sounded like it. But Jasmine couldn't see who she was talking to so she tried to get through the group of tourists to find Cerys, after apologising to the family she had been talking with, for abruptly ending their small talk.

She could hear Cerys' distinctive voice coming back towards her.

"See you at the Luau soon then, oh what fun this will be".

As Cerys came into Jasmine's sight, Cerys was waving at a group of males who were waving back at her, but Jasmine couldn't make out who they were.

" Oi, where have you been? What have you been up to and who were those people?" demanded Jasmine.

"So many questions, keep your drawers on".

Their shuttle arrived and they got on.

"So?" asked Jasmine.

"Remember those blokes at Cardiff Airport that I was talking with and I said one of them was asking about you, well, they are staying at a hotel near to ours and they are going to the Luau too….ahhhh….Jazz this could be your night", squawked Cerys.

"Oh no, Cerys, please I just want to spend a quiet and relaxing holiday with you. Why have you got to spoil it", said Jasmine disappointingly.

"Oh don't be so miserable, it will be fun, honestly". Cerys pulled Jasmine in front of her and gave her a pouting but playful smile.

"Alright, don't expect anything to happen because it WON'T, you daft mare". They both giggled like teenagers.

Chapter 9

Jasmine and Cerys arrived at Paradise Cove Luau grounds just as the Luau had started. They were a bit disappointed as the receptionist at their hotel had told them, as they were leaving for the evening, that the whale watching, dolphin watching and turtle watching trip that they had booked for the following morning, had been overbooked and they couldn't go. They decided that they would look at what other trip they could book instead the next morning.

Gorgeous red, orange, pink and blue hues left them and the other guests in awe as the sun made its way toward the horizon, across the ocean behind them. The ubiquitous sunshine that had provided twelve hours of life-giving light and beach and outdoor fun sank peacefully into the sea as if being tucked in after a hard day's work. The seated area and the stage area were surrounded by flame flickering lanterns. The air smelled of the ocean, flora and mouth-watering flavours of the forthcoming feast. Jasmine and Cerys headed towards the complimentary drinks table where they were given Mai Tai greetings in huge cocktail glasses by a very petite waitress who was wearing none other than a very predictable, but traditional costume of a coconut shell bra and a grass skirt. She also gave them each a fresh flower lei and graciously placed them over their heads so the flowers fell perfectly over their shoulders.

As they glugged their cocktails down, the girls headed quickly towards a table that was near to the stage and the Tiki bar. The tables were filling up quickly and they wanted to make sure they had a good spot. Music was playing in the background, the sound of ukuleles filled the air.

"This is wonderful", said Jasmine.

"It truly is, now drink up girl, let's get another one in before the bar gets full", replied Cerys.

Jasmine tutted, rolled her eyes and sipped the rest of her cocktail.

Cerys came back from the bar with two more glasses of Mai Tai just as the food was being served. The Luau pit pig had been dug up from the underground oven from the Imu amphitheatre and had been shredded, placed in wooden bowls and was being served to the guests with a selection of poke, a raw, colourful salad and lomi salmon, fresh salmon with tomato, onion and Hawaiian chilli pepper. It smelled and looked divine.

As the girls chatted, giggled and devoured their delicious meal, a waiter, male this time, dressed only in a grass skirt served them a large jug of beer and two large glasses, (lager to the Brits).

"Sorry love, we haven't ordered that", said Jasmine whilst she was trying to swallow a piece of very chewy pork.

"It's from the gentlemen at the table back there", he said as he pointed into the darkness.

He scurried off before the girls could ask him anything else.

"Oh, well....cheers, why do people giving us free drinks? I'm not complaining mind you, but it's very odd. Once we have finished our meals, shall we go and investigate?" asked Jasmine.

"Yea it is a bit strange. I'm not leaving our table until the show is over though, someone will nick our seats", said Cerys as she craned her neck and pursed her lips at the same time, trying to see if she could catch the eye of the mysterious drinks buyer.

The girls couldn't eat dessert as they were so full so the waiter told them they would box it up for them to take way later. It was a coconut based dessert called Haupia and the smell of creaminess of the coconut wafted around them in the cool evening breeze as it was being served to the other guests who obviously hadn't stuffed themselves like the girls had.

As the main stage lit up for the show, the girls couldn't relax, both kept looking casually over their shoulders, both suspicious and wary, probably due to the jobs they did.

"Hope it's not drugged" said Jasmine as she sniffed the jug of beer.

"Can't be" sniggered Cerys, as she poured herself a glass and took a sip.

"Tastes fine c'mon have some", she giggled as she poured Jasmine a glass.

"It's a nice gesture from someone, we are two BEAUTIFUL ladies, who wouldn't want to buy us a drink", Cerys crowed in a loud voice and raised her glass to the darkness as if to say,

"Cheers".

Once the hula dancers, fire eaters and limbo dancers had finished their sets on stage, a Hawaiian band started to play and people started to get up and dance to the music.

Cerys stood up, straightened up her stunning strapless, white, tight fitted dress by pulling it up from the top and adjusting the hem, grabbed hold of Jasmine's hand and gestured her towards the dance area. Jasmine was wearing a Grecian style dress, fuchsia with a deep v- neckline, with a draw string waist and it was just about the knee. They both kicked off their sandals as they headed away from the table. Jasmine's hair was loose and flowing as she and Cerys danced and sang along with Frankie Valli's "Can't take my eyes off you".

Everyone sang the chorus and everyone, except a few men propping up the tiki bar, seemed to be up and dancing. The atmosphere was wonderful.

"Oh let's have a paddle shall we and check out who bought us the drinks as we pass by", said Cerys.

"Yea, why not, I have a bit of a stitch after all that food and dancing around".

All the tables near the back of the seating area were empty. They both looked around to see if anyone had noticed them exploring but everyone was dancing and no-one seemed to be interested in them. They both shrugged their shoulders.

"Oh well", said Cery's

They linked arms as they ambled tipsily towards the water. The band was still playing in the background and the other guests were still dancing to, "Livin La Vida Loca".

As the pair childishly started to splash water at each other with their feet, a man's voice came out of the darkness. It was deep, sexy and had a type of a North American twang.

"Well hello ladies", he said in a smooth, velvety tone. As the girls looked up, all they could see was a silhouette of a man, they couldn't see his face. Cerys took a step backwards in surprise and let out an almighty scream and fell face down into the sand clutching her foot.

The man took a step forward, neither of the girls looked up to see his face in time and he shouted,

"Stay there, I'll get help".

Chapter 10

"It's okay, don't worry Ma'am", said one of the waiters from the Luau as he and one of the entertainers helped carry Cerys back to the seating area. They lifted her foot to discover she had stepped on a jelly fish. A small group of guests from the Luau had started to gather around the girls. Some were making "ouch" faces, some were covering their mouths after gasping at the sight.

"Okay ladies and gents, back to the party, nothing to see here, go enjoy yourselves", said Koka, the waiter who was tending to Cerys. The group disbursed.

"Ow ow ow", cried Cerys. "Please help me, it bloody kills".

Koka removed the small tentacles of the jelly fish with a shell, then he signalled to another waiter, Lopaka, to get some sea water to rinse it.

"I feel sick and dizzy", winced Cerys as she squeezed Jasmine's hand.

"You will be fine Ma'am, we have tended to these types of incidents on many an occasion", said Koka.

Lopaka then came from the kitchen area, once he had emptied a large cup of sea water over Cery's foot, carrying heated water, vinegar and papaya....and a meat tenderizer!!!

"Owwwwww-aaaah", screamed Cerys, as Koka administered the strange concoction over the sting. Jasmine had never seen her like this, she was always the courageous one.

"Do you have ibuprofen?" asked Lopaka

"Not on me, it's back at the hotel room", answered Jasmine.

"I suggest you go back to your hotel, take some painkillers and take a fifteen to a twenty minute hot shower and this will deactivate the venom of this jellyfish and you must then rest. You must come back for another Luau when you are better, please stay away from the ocean though, and it will be complimentary, on us", chuckled Lopaka.

"Thank you so much for all your help, so sorry to spoil the evening", sniffed Cerys, with tears and mascara streaming down her cheeks.

"You are welcome Ma'am, if you are still unwell, speak with the reception at your hotel and they will help you but you should be fine, it's not a deadly jellyfish that you squashed," replied Koka with a sarcastic, beaming smile.

The girls gathered their shoes and headed back to their hotel, more sober than they were before "the incident", but slightly and quietly annoyed they didn't find out who bought their drinks, and who the mysterious stranger was on the beach that went to fetch help.

"I'm glad they didn't pee on you like Joey and Chandler did when Monica was stung by a jelly fish in that episode of 'Friends', giggled Jasmine.

"Aahh that feels better", sighed Cerys as she emerged from the shower in a big, white fluffy bathrobe, still with a smudge of mascara evident under each eye.

"Sorry to spoil the evening mate, typical of me eh? I am really pissed off with myself", said Cerys in anger as she gulped back two painkillers with a glass of water.

"Don't be such a silly moo, you didn't do it on purpose. We'll get a good night's sleep and if you feel alright tomorrow we'll go and relax on the beach and then have a wander around the shops to find some masks for the Halloween parade for Saturday, shall we? Not sure what other trip I want to do instead of the whale watching do you?"

"Nah... we'll have a look again. Come yer. I love you mate, you know that don't you", said Cerys as she gave Jasmine a hug, (or a Cwtch as the Welsh say).

"I'm not going in the sea for a swim though, pool only for me from now on", she whispered in her mate's ear.

The sun was a beautiful burnt orange and a golden yellow colour and the temperature was in the low eighties as Jasmine and Cerys headed towards the beachfront, which was a short walk from their hotel. Cerys, feeling much better, with only a small red lump on her foot to show for her drama, wore a cotton white t-shirt over her sexy turquoise bikini and very skimpy denim shorts and Jasmine wore a lemon coloured beach dress over a matching coloured tankini.

They sunbathed, read, laughed, chatted and enjoyed a session of one of their favourite games, people watching, as the pale, clear, blue Pacific Ocean lapped against the white, soft sand.

"Look at that fella over by there", secretly pointed Jasmine.

The man, dressed in just black shorts, was walking up and down the shoreline, on his own, gesturing and nodding his head.

"Is he schizophrenic or is he wearing a blue tooth thingy?"

They both laughed out loud.

"Seems to have brought his packed lunch with him too as she sighted a suspicious bulge inside his shorts", scoffed Jasmine.

"Look, look", whispered Cerys.

"Where?" asked Jasmine

"That hot looking mamma bending and stretching near the rails, over there. Real or false boobies? I'd say false, as I've seen many in my time and they don't move like that. I wouldn't mind finding out though. Aww knickers, she has a man friend. Oh well".

Jasmine tutted, whilst shaking her head and smiling.

"What?" replied Cerys.

"Ooo, that couple there", Cerys gestured with her head as a male in his forties, body the shape of a capital D, wearing an ill-fitting beige t-shirt over budgie smuggling swimming trunks that were so tight, his religion was in full view. He was puffing on a cigar, and a very slim, toned woman who was with him, possibly in her late twenties, wearing a black bikini top and matching thong bottoms, placed their towels and beach bags near to the girls.

"Trophy wife or daughter?" asked Cerys.

"We'll soon know if he grabs her ass", laughed Jasmine.

They both watched on secretly from behind their sunglasses as the woman straddled the man, as he took off his t-shirt and laid face down on the towel and then she rubbed and caressed sun lotion into his vast back. He was moaning with pleasure as she rocked her pelvis, rubbing herself against his backside as she massaged the cream in to his skin.

"Gross, get a room, defo a trophy wife...I would hope so anyway", muttered Cerys.

As the girls gathered their belongings, late in the afternoon, they shook the sand out of their towels and picked up their flip flops, a man's voice shouted,

"Hello ladies".

The girls stood up and searched around to see three men, all fairly decent looking, (thought Jasmine), walking towards them.

"Oh...Hiya", replied Cerys excitedly.

"These are the guys from the airport and the Pearl Harbour trip I told you about Jaz, what are you doing yer boys, are you stalking us?" Cerys said coquettishly.

"Ha! Funny, nope we were just taking a walk, taking in the scenery, ya know, how about you... you leaving ladies?"

Said the one male, who was about six foot tall, late thirties, mid brown, wavy, hair, tanned, very attractive, very well-toned, wearing a white vest top and navy, tight shorts and flip flops that he was carrying in his one hand.

"Yep, we don't want our skins to look like leather, and we don't want to watch any more of the floor show over there", Cerys gestured towards the Capital D man and his woman.

"We are off to check out the shops to look at some costumes and masks for the Halloween parade on Saturday...oh by the way this is my best mate Jasmine",

Cerys pulled Jasmine's arm and pushed her forward as if presenting her as a prize. Jasmine tugged her arm away, gave her friend a sneaky frown and quietly and shyly said,

"Hello".

The other two males were also quite attractive, both late thirties, early forties, one was about five foot ten, fit looking, not as toned as the first male, dark but slightly greying, short, hair with a goatee beard, wearing a thin t-shirt with a pale blue, faded Hollister logo on the front, black, just above the knee shorts and sporty sandals. The third male was slightly shorter, about five foot eight, blonde, short on the sides but a bit of a flowing coif on top, a bit like a James Dean style, very clean shaven, thicker set but still fit looking, with just a pair of dark green cargo shorts on, flip flops in his hands and a black t-shirt hanging from his back pocket. All of them had North American accents.

The males all stood staring and chuckling for a while at the capital D man and his woman, before returning their attention back to the girls.

"So, the Halloween parade, fancy meeting up afterwards then ladies for a drink?", asked the tallest one as he winked at Cerys and who announced his name as Joe, the one with the greying hair was Dylan and the one with the James Dean hair was Rick.

'He's barking up the wrong tree there', thought Jasmine to herself, but Cerys winked back flirtatiously.

"Perhaps the tides have changed", again thought Jasmine as she smiled to herself.

"What do you think babes? Shall we meet these gents for a pint or two", Cerys nudged Jasmine.

"Yes, go on then why not, how about that bar and grill that overlooks the golf course, Lei Lei's bar I think it's called and it's not too far for us to stumble back to the hotel after wards is it Cerys?", Jasmine laughed, feeling a bit flushed and a bit embarrassed after she had said it.

"Great, but we will have a few more of our buddies with us if that's okay ladies, we are here on a type of reunion but we will try not to be rowdy", announced Rick.

The men each kissed Jasmine and Cery's hand as they walked off and waved and shouted,

"See ya Saturday ladies, you Brits can teach us how to drink no doubt".

"Oh my Gawd", said Jasmine. "What are we doing? What are YOU doing, I'm too old and...and?"

"And what? It's just a bit of fun girlie, stop blushing for feck sake, you may lose your virginity again if you play your cards right, I may try a different sport, if you know what I mean...only joking I am", Cerys laughed as they headed off to the little row of shops near to the beach for their Halloween outfits, pushing and shoving each other in jest as they walked along.

Jasmine secretly cringing and blushing as they went.

Chapter 11

Halloween wasn't until the Monday but the main, local celebrations and parade were being held on the Saturday before, but the local children still went out Trick or Treating for candy on the thirty-first of October.

It was Saturday morning, the weather was overcast with a cool breeze, and the girls went for breakfast at the North Shore Kula Grill restaurant at their resort. Both of them were feeling peckish so they both went for the breakfast buffet. Cerys started with granola, yoghurt and honey, then went on to have pancakes, scrambled eggs, bacon and finished with some fresh fruit. Jasmine went for oatmeal, eggs benedict and finished off with a plate of watermelon and berries.....and the never ending refills of coffee.

All through breakfast Cerys kept checking her mobile, whilst looking a bit anxious but trying to conceal it from Jasmine.

"What's going on?" asked Jasmine as she scooped her last bit of her eggs benedict into her mouth.

"Are you expecting a call or something?"

"Just checking to see if dad or Steph have tried to contact me that's all", replied Cerys sharply, whilst still checking her phone again.

"So, looking forward to tonight, seeing all those handsome guys?" said Cerys changing the subject and her tone quickly.

"Um...sort of, but.....oh you know what I'm like...I'm shy and always act goofy when I meet anyone new, especially those of the male species. I would prefer it if it was just us really Cerys".

"You will be fine, and I'll tell you what, if you feel uncomfortable, just say and we'll make a sharp exit".

"Okay, you promise though, cos I know what you're like, you've said things like that before and then you change your mind about leaving or staying".

"I promise", replied Cerys in a childlike voice.

After their hearty breakfast the girls decided that, as the weather wasn't too good for sunbathing, they would have a day of pampering before their night out, at the Nalu kinetic spa which was also at their resort.

According to the brochure the spa provided a multi-sensory experience of the ocean: dramatic window walls with views of legendary swells, the sound of surf crashing on the beach, and an innovative Wave Therapy massage table that gently rocks you as if you were floating. Warm salt stones calm you down after an adrenalin surge, and a line of marine-infused products show tenderness to skin and hair that has been exposed to sun, sand and salt.

The girls lay face down on massage couches which were next to each other, with towels covering just their backsides and the tops of their legs. The massage therapists blended oils and rubbed deep into their shoulders then down to towards the spine.

Cerys groaned, "This is heaven, pure heaven".

Jasmine didn't think the same. Her massage therapist, who was tall, athletic looking, had over done it with the blusher, three inch black roots emerging from her bleached blonde hair that was tied up in a top knot bun, dug her thumbs and elbows in to her muscles so hard that Jasmine yelped several times.

"Please can you not dig so hard, you are hurting me?" asked Jasmine politely.

Cerys opened one eye to see what was going on. Her therapist was, petite, wearing very subtle and natural makeup, had long, dark, shiny hair that was also tied up in a top knot bun. She was gentle and soothing when she circled her thumbs into Cerys' upper back.

"Sorry zer is more meat on you zan your friend and I need to get deep in tizzues for dis to work and you feel benefit", replied Jasmine's therapist, in a German accent and broken English as she proceeded to dig even deeper.

Cerys giggled and mouthed quietly to Jasmine "Cheeky cow".

After the massage the girls were treated to a therapy that used warm salt stones, placed strategically on various muscles.

"Ouch", cried out Jasmine as the last stone her therapist placed on the base of her neck was red hot but was then quickly removed by the woman as she muttered something in German under her breath. All the others had been warm and comforting up until that one. Both therapists left the room to let the girls relax but they could be heard arguing outside the door.

"Jeez old snooty knickers didn't like you did she?" sniggered Cerys.

"I know, what was that about? Do I have a fat back?" she asked Cerys.

"No you don't you are bloody gorgeous, take no notice of that miserable tit, she must have been kicked out of bed the wrong side", replied Cerys sleepily.

The girls made their way back to their hotel suite after their afternoon at the spa. Cerys felt soothed and relaxed but Jasmine felt as if she had gone ten rounds with a world champion heavyweight boxer.

"I need a bubble bath and a very large drink", exclaimed Jasmine as she dropped her bag on the floor and lead across the plush sofa in their luxurious hotel suite.

"How about I order some room service? Some cocktails and snacks whilst you soak your backside in the tub, and I think I will make a complaint against that bitch too", Cerys said whilst stroking Jasmines hair as she sat next to her on the arm of the sofa.

"Sounds bloody wonderful, but don't say anything about her, forget it. I don't think I will go there again though. I'm not fussed on strangers touching me anyway", Jasmine yawned.

As Cerys opened the hotel room door for the waiter to bring in the trolley that had a large, full to the brim, jug of Long Island iced tea cocktail, bottle of wine and a selection nibbles and snacks, she noticed the massage therapist, that poor Jasmine had the misfortune to encounter, walk passed the door. Both glared at each other, not blinking.

"What's your problem love?" she shouted after the woman as she stepped outside the room. The woman kept walking but turned to keep eye contact as she walked on.

Cerys tipped the waiter and then shut the door behind him.

"Guess who I just saw?" squealed Cerys and she pushed the bathroom door with her knee whilst carrying two large, full cocktails glasses.

"Ummm....George Clooney?" asked Jasmine sarcastically, as she emerged from under the bubbles in the bath tub, hair dripping wet.

"Hope you told him to sprawl across my bed and wait for me naked with a rose between his teeth".

She reached for the cocktail glass and took a sip.

"Only that cow that assaulted you at the spa, she walked passed the hotel room, giving me the evils as she went by. I could have gladly punched her lights out".

"May be you can order a massage from room service and someone has requested her services, I dunno, strange though. Anyway, pass me that towel girlie, let's get ready for a good night out", smiled Jasmine, whilst savouring the luscious taste of the cocktail.

"Well you've changed your tune", said a surprised Cerys as she threw Jasmine her towel and headed off to her room to get ready, taking a handful of nibbles and her drink with her.

As they both drained the last few drops of their cocktail glasses, Jasmine twirled around in her black, tight jeans and black, long sleeved fitted t-shirt and wedged heels.

"Well, does my back look fat in this?" she quizzed Cerys

Cerys smacked her backside then gave her a cuddle.

"You smell and look beautiful", she said as she gently tucked a strand of loose hair behind Jasmine's ear in a motherly way.

"You look pretty damn hot too", remarked Jasmine.

They picked up their Halloween masks, which were both full faced masquerade ball masks, both in red with devil horns on top with an elastic strap around the back to keep them in place, grabbed their handbags and Cerys put the bottle of wine in the cooler for later. She took a couple of tablets from her handbag and swallowed them quickly.

"What's that, what are you taking, oh Gawd Cerys, you are not taking drugs are you, oh Gawd".

"Painkillers for period pain you daft bugger, you know how I hate drugs, why would I take drugs, l love life, and I love you too now move your butt...tsk...drugs". Cerys said as she pushed Jasmine out of the door into the beautiful, lush green grounds of their hotel.

"Sorry are you okay?" mouthed Jasmine.

"Yes....now c'mon".

Cerys, who was also wearing black jeans, an off the shoulder, three quarter length sleeved top and black low heeled shoes, kissed Jasmine on the cheek and playfully skipped and wiggled off in front of her.

Chapter 12

The sun had disappeared off into the horizon and there was a cool breeze blowing the tropical and exotic plants and trees and long bladed grass. The main street near to the resort was lit with different coloured lights of all shapes and sizes and the stores had each decorated their windows with displays of ghouls and ghosties and monsters. Locals and tourists alike had gathered along the sidewalks, all dressed in costumes and masks, swaying, clapping and moving to the sound of various marching bands. Groups of people shaking buckets for any odd change for charity lined the roads and danced along to the different beats of the bands. The atmosphere was electric.

Jasmine and Cerys found a spot next to a family of three who were all dressed as evil pumpkins. The little girl, who was sat on her dad's shoulder kept grabbing one of Cery's horns on her mask, giggling each time Cerys made out she was going to grab her hand. The mother kept telling her off every time she went for the horn but this made her giggle and jump about even more.

The parade could be heard coming along the road in the distance and everyone started clapping and whistling and whooping. The first group to be seen were dressed as zombies and werewolves and they were performing Michael Jackson's 'Thriller'. They acted out the dance and different scenes as they moved along the road, occasionally jumping in front of people to make them scream.

As they moved off the next group of entertainers appeared, dressed as Dracula, Frankenstein, more werewolves, witches and warlocks dancing to "The Monster Mash".

They moved on followed by a mixture of Freddy Krugers dancing to Jazzy Jeff and the Fresh Prince's song "Night mare on my Street".

The little girl next to Cerys had climbed down from her dad's shoulders and was clinging tightly to his chest as he held her in his arms. She was covering her eyes with her hands, peeking every now and then through her fingers.

As the parade came to an end, the spectators were encouraged to join in and follow the parade that led to a fairground and BBQ on the beach. Cerys and Jasmine joined in and walked behind the family they had been stood next too.

The drums were beating, people were still dancing, the girls joined in singing along to the "Ghostbusters" theme.

"If there's something strange in your neighbourhood, who gonna call....GHOSTBUSTERS", everyone sang out loud.

"I'm having a great time", shouted Jasmine to Cerys.

"Me too mate", Cerys sang back as she span around and waved her hands in the air to the music.

There was a sudden surge of people from behind the girls and a rowdy commotion echoed towards them. Cerys stumbled but steadied herself swiftly, then a man was pushed into the back of her.

"Sorry ma'am", the man said as he grabbed Cerys quickly to stop her stumbling again.

As Jasmine went to take hold of Cery's hand, there was an even bigger surge from behind and the girls became separated. Cerys was pushed on ahead and Jasmine had a job to stand up. The force of people behind was too much to bare and she suddenly collapsed. Curling up in a ball in the middle of the road to shelter her head, Jasmine screamed out Cerys' name at the top of her lungs. A strong arm pulled her from the ground on to her feet and dragged her out of the road, the person wouldn't let go, they kept pulling and dragging her into a side road which was pitch black, not a light in sight. The rowdiness and music could be heard in the distance. Jasmine cried out,

"Stop...please", but the person kept pulling her.

All sorts of horror stories flashed through her mind. Was she going to be robbed, raped or even worse, killed?

The person stopped and pushed Jasmine's face up against the wall.

"Thank you for pulling me off the road", said Jasmine pitifully.

"SHAD UP, you stupid beech". It was a woman and she had the same accent as the massage therapist from the spa.

She grabbed a handful of Jasmine's hair and pulled her head back with one hand, still pushing her body forwards in to the wall. Then she pushed what felt like a gun into her back.

Jasmine was absolutely terrified but tried to keep her cool. She held out her hands either side in surrender.

"Take my bag, take everything, but please don't hurt me", she whispered desperately.

"I said SHUD UP". She bashed Jasmine's head into the wall.

She could feel a trickle of blood falling over her left eye under her mask. Her heart began to race and her breathing was rapid. She felt as if she was going to pass out.

The woman was silent for a bit, she seemed to sniff Jasmine's hair, then she pushed her on the ground on her knees.

Jasmine began to shake with fear, she felt sick, tears streamed down her cheeks. What the hell did this woman want and why had she taken a strong dislike to her.

The woman put what again felt like a gun again to the back of Jasmine's head. She pushed it into her skull then drew it down to the back of her neck.

"Does your neck still hurts beech from zer hot stone? I hope it does. You have ruined my life. You know why you have done zis, huh?" she quizzed as she pushed the object back into Jasmine's head.

"No, I don't know you, I don't know what I've done. Please, you have the wrong person. I haven't done anything. Please let me go", begged Jasmine.

"Ha, you know damn well, you got zer man I want, my man, not yours, to meet you here on zis middle of no-ver Island. I followed him, he wants you, I heard him, hacked his computer, checked his phone. He is mine not yours". She pushed the object harder into the back of Jasmine's head.

"I don't know what you mean, what man? I'm here with my friend, you saw her at the spa, I'm not meeting anyone, I'm begging you", whimpered Jasmine.

Cerys made it out of the crowd safely. She was frantically trying to find her friend. She walked on the sidewalk back up towards the last place she saw her before they were separated. The roads were still busy but people had started to disperse.

"JASMINE....JAZ, where are you?" she yelled.

She rang her mobile but it rang a few time but went to voice mail.

"Are you okay ma'am?" a Police Officer approached her as she searched groups of people for her friend.

"I lost my friend when the parade got out of control. I can't find her."

"Sorry about that ma'am. Two rival gangs decided to come into town for some rich pickings from tourists like yourselves. One eyewitness said they saw a tall blonde woman wearing a bat girl mask, dressed all in black and extremely high heels, like fetish shoes the witness said, whatever they are, playing gang members off against each other, flirting with them and goading them to fight each other. We have a description of her and we have put out an APB for her. We have arrested the main offenders for fighting. What is the description of your friend and my colleagues and I will keep a look out for her? Where are you staying Ma'am, can I give you a ride back?".

Cerys gave him Jasmine's description but declined a ride back to the hotel as she thought she would make her way to Lei Lei's bar, where they had arranged to meet the guys and their mates from the beach. Maybe Jasmine had gone there.

She rushed into the bar, her mask in her hand, mobile in the other with her handbag over her shoulder. She searched the faces in the crowded bar for her friend. A hand touched her shoulder.

"Hey, hi", said a familiar voice, "You made it then, where's your friend? We have been waiting for a serious drinking contest, Brits versus the Yanks and the Canadians.

"Hi Joe...I've lost Jasmine, we were separated when the parade went out of control. I was pushed forward and then I lost her. I've searched the streets and thought she may have made her way here". She was out of breath. She tried ringing her on her mobile again, but still no reply.

"Let me get you a drink", said Joe as he steered her towards a group of his mates.

They all stood up to greet her but she just held her hand up to say "hi", and turned back towards the door with her mobile phone close to her ear, trying to ring her friend again.

One of the group of males followed her, after Joe had told them all what had happened.

"Cerys, Cerys", he shouted after her.

"Good to meet you, finally," he hugged her.

"Oh Gawd, hiya, sorry, I didn't mean to be rude, I'm so worried, where could she be".

"We will help you find her, don't worry, she probably just took a wrong turn", he said in his throaty North American voice.

"Stop lying to me you English beech, I know I tell you... I know". Screeched the woman as she again pulled Jasmine's hair and again forced her head into the wall.

"I'm bloody Welsh for your information, and I don't know what you are bloody talking about you crazy woman", yelled Jasmine in a fit of fury. She had started to get angry with the pushing and shoving of a mad woman

"Hey, what's going on....hey you leave her alone", shouted a man's voice from the distance.

"You stay a-vay from zer Skipper or I will kills you and your sh-tupid bimbo friend." She whispered in Jasmines ear before pushing her and running off in the opposite direction.

Jasmine tried to get up on her feet but her knees had gone stiff with fear.

"Are you okay?" said a woman's voice as she ran towards her.

The man that was with her tried to run after the mad woman but he lost her. He reached Jasmine the same time as the woman.

They shone a novelty torch in her face that they had bought from a stall that was set out for the parade. As she removed her mask, blood trickled furiously down face from a cut her above her eye.

"Aw it's you, we met you at Cardiff airport, remember, let's get you somewhere safe".

The couple, Mia and Max, were the honeymoon couple that sat next to Jasmine at the airport on the way out to LA. As they made their way out into the main street, Mia gave Jasmine a tissue that she had pulled from her handbag, to wipe the blood and tears from her face.

Jasmine felt as if she was going to pass out as the couple sat her down on the curb by the sidewalk, quizzing her about what happened.

"Did that person hurt you? Was it a man or a woman? Looked like a woman to me as they ran off from me? She looked like she was limping, did you see their face?" asked Max.

"It…it was a woman... she works at the spa at the hotel....she... she was crazy, am sure she had a gun, I didn't see it, she held something pointy in my back and head...I dunno... feel sick".

The couple helped her up and took her back to the hotel reception, where they contacted the local police. After she had given her statement, the couple took her to the lobby bar.

"Shit, Cerys, oops", Jasmine suddenly remembered after a brandy and four "blow jobs"!!!!

She had read a book about a group of women who visited a burlesque club for a hen party and one of the cocktails they had was called a "blow job". It was a mixture of Baileys, Amaretto topped off with whipped cream. She had persuaded the barman to make them for her rescuers and herself.

"Cerys...s'mmee, have been mugged by a crazy Germans"

Slurred Jasmine as she rang Cerys on her mobile.

"Jeez, Jasmine, are you okay, you sound terrible, are you hurt, where are you?" Cerys replied with relief whilst mouthing the words, "Jasmine, she's been mugged", to the group of male searchers that were with her.

"Whaaa?" asked Jasmine. "Aw mate am with M and M have had a brandy and four blow jobs, am totally wasted"

"You what? Where are you? I'm coming to get you", Cerys worriedly enquired, thinking she has been assaulted by a rapper who forced Jasmine to give oral sex.

"Am about two miles away but if you hurry you can do it in one, ...hic...hee hee...am so tipsy, see you in our room...love you..mwoah...mwoah", replied Jasmine as she blew kisses down the phone to Cerys, and promptly fell backwards off her stool after she announced to Max and Mia how suddenly relaxed she felt.

Chapter 13

Cerys sat next to Jasmine in her room, holding her hand whilst she slept and snored.

Max and Mia had given her the full story to Cerys when she had arrived along with a few of the guys from Lei Lei's bar. Between them, Mia and Max and the reception staff had managed to carry Jasmine to her room.

"I'll call you and arrange something", Cerys whispered to the guys from the bar as they left with Max and Mia.

Jasmine suddenly woke from her slumber, gasping for air.

"Shush, It's okay, I'm here beaut, don't worry", Cerys climbed on the bed next to Jasmine and gently stroked her forehead avoiding the plaster that covered the cut.

"Cerys, oh Gawd", cried Jasmine as she sat up and pulled Cerys towards her, hugging her tightly to her chest.

"I felt a warm breath over my face, I thought it was her".

"Shush, it's okay, the doors are locked, hotel security are patrolling around the area, you are safe, here, have some water,"

Cerys lifted a glass of water to Jasmine's lips.

"She told me to stay away from someone called 'zer Skipper', I don't know what she was talking about, she said she would kill us if we didn't", sobbed Jasmine.

Cerys pulled her into her arms and cradled her until she dropped back off to sleep. She pulled the sheet around her shoulders as she lay her head gently on the pillow.

"It's me", said Cerys as she crept out of Jasmine's room, clutching her mobile phone close to her ear.

"She told Jasmine she was going to kill us both if we didn't stay away from Zer Skipper", she murmured.

"Okay, alright, cheers for that let me know, speak soon", she replied to the person at the other end of the phone.

Jasmine awoke as it was starting to get light outside. Her head was thumping. She reached for the glass of water that was on the bedside cabinet and saw that Cerys was curled up on the bed next her. Slowly remembering the incident from the night before, Jasmine felt the cut on her forehead. She frowned and winced at the mild pain she felt from it, whilst still trying to understand what the hell went on.

"Hey, you're awake, how do you feel", yawned Cerys sympathetically.

"I feel like some crazy woman scared the shit out of me with a gun and bashed my head into a wall. Why? I don't know....have we dealt with her in work at the police station for something and she has followed us, flown over here to get her own back? Would someone follow someone to Hawaii to get their own back? I don't know. Why would she do this? I think I want to go home", rambled Jasmine rapidly asking and answering her own questions, as she climbed out of bed and proceeded to pack her suitcase. Her heart was racing again, she began to breathe heavily, then ran to the bathroom to throw up.

Whilst she was in the bathroom there was a knock at the hotel room door. Cerys called out to see who it was.

"It's security ma'am, the police are here".

Cerys opened the door to a male and female police officer. She spoke to them for a while about the incident and then Jasmine strolled out of the bathroom in a white fluffy robe, clutching a piece of loo roll to her mouth, hair tied up in a ponytail, to find out where the voices were coming from. They were both sat on the sofa in the suite.

"Hello Ms Williams. We have apprehended the female that we believe assaulted you ma'am. We spoke with the therapists at the spa where she worked and they have identified her from the mug shot we showed them. Also the eyewitnesses from the parade gave a description and the details matched, although she had a mask on, the details of her clothing were the same as what we found when we searched her room at the guest house she was staying at. We also searched her room and work locker for weapons but didn't find anything, also swabbed her hands for any residue in case she fired a gun at any time. We couldn't find anything. I know from you statement you didn't mention any gun being fired but we checked anyway.

We have been contacted by another party on the island who also had unwanted attention from this woman and again they have fully identified her. We have made a record of this as well. We will not need to see you again, unless you really want to go to court to give evidence, which could be a while away until we get the date. We have enough evidence to prosecute her, you will not be required to stand as a witness at this stage, and as you are on vacation we would not want detain you here any longer than is necessary. You are safe and free to enjoy the rest of your stay. We have all your particulars so if we need to speak to you when you go back home or if you are required to give evidence in court at a later date, we can arrange a video link to you back home. Is there anything else we can tell you ma'am?" said the extremely tall male Police Officer.

"Yes, who was she and why did she take a dislike to me, I want to know?"... exclaimed Jasmine angrily trying to take it all in.

"Her name is Astrid Braun and she has been moving around and doing various jobs in the States and Canada, working as therapist and doing some bar work. She is unstable and...", the officer looked at Cerys then back to Jasmine, "she has an obsessive, compulsive, personality disorder stated on her previous record. She gets fixated with people and imagines all sorts, it seems she just took a dislike to you for some reason. It can happen like that." replied the officer.

A message came over the Police Officer's radios, the female officer acknowledged the call.

"We have to go but here is my card, if there is anything else, I mean anything you need to speak to us about, then please don't hesitate to contact me or the office. Enjoy your vacation".

Cerys showed them to the door and the male officer looked at Cerys, winked and whispered,

"Good luck".

"I fancy a coffee, do you?" asked Cerys.

Jasmine nodded.

"Shall I go and get some from the lobby, whilst you unpack?"

Cerys smiled hopefully.

"Yeah go on then", Jasmine replied with a sigh of relief.

Chapter 14

To move on from the "second incident", the first being the jellyfish sting, and enjoy the rest of their holiday, the girls booked a day trip to Maui. It was four thirty in the morning and their transport to the airport was picking them up at five O'clock in the morning. Both were tired but excited at the same time.

"Camera, money, sunglasses, passports for identification, booking form receipts, sun cream, towels, lippy, what else do we need?" Jasmine fussed as she slipped her feet into her comfy walking shoes whilst checking her bag at the same time.

They had been told when they booked the trip to take their passports as the names on the booking forms had to be exactly the same as on their photo identifications, as it was a necessity for the Transport Security Administration. This organization was created in response to the September 11th 2001 attacks.

"I think that's all we need babes, ooh a light weight waterproof jacket, just in case we get a bit of rain, I'll go and fetch them", replied Cerys.

She collected their jackets and took a couple of tablets from her bag and swallowed them down quickly without Jasmine seeing and questioning her.

"Ready", she announced as she walked out of her bedroom.

They both wore shorts, with t-shirts, Cerys tied a thin cream cardigan around her waist and slung her bag across her shoulders. Jasmine put her hoodie into her enormous and filled to the brim beach bag. She had everything from mosquito spray to tampons buried in there.

They flew to Maui in a small plane with a bunch of other tourists that had booked the same trip. That was an experience in itself the girls thought. Although it was small, compact and bumpy the magnificent views outweighed all of the uncomfortableness they endured.

They were met in Maui by a tour guide and a mini bus. His name was Ted, (the tour guide, not the mini bus), and he was dressed in a smart green uniform with long shorts and a baseball cap.

"Aloha, Welcome, welcome", said Ted as he ushered the tourists on to the mini bus.

The other tourists consisted of a group of three ladies, Linda, Alison and Sue, all in their late sixties, dressed in a mixture of floral tops, low cut cleavage tops and shorts, with wide brimmed hats and huge sunglasses all clucking and clacking and chattering like a load of chickens that had just been told some exciting news. They were like the Golden Girls. There was another couple, a man and a woman, who were very quiet and very clingy with each other, grasping to each other's arms as if they were going to the gallows. They didn't speak, just nodded. Last of all there was a very polite Japanese couple in their late twenties who took photos of everything from the mini bus to the Red Crested Cardinal bird that had landed on a Kapok tree nearby.

"Are you settled folks?" asked Ted

"Yes", everyone shouted with glee.

"Okay, off we go". Ted shut the door tightly on the minibus got into the driver's seat and pressed a very impressive little speaker button on the dash board that he had said he had installed so that everyone could hear him speak as he drove along.

"Okay folks, welcome to Maui. We are going to take a journey of a lifetime to East Maui. This all day tour will take you around a beautiful region of the "Magic Isle", showing you some of the most scenic spots found on any of the Hawaiian Islands. It's a sixty eight mile round trip so make yourself comfortable and if you need a refreshment stop, just let me know", Ted announced over his speaker.

He went on to say, "There are more than six hundred curves in the road to Hana. We will weave through the surrounding forest and cross a total of fifty nine bridges whilst making our way along the eastern coast of the island."

"Oooooh", said the three ladies in harmony.

Ted continued. "It does take time to navigate the route so sit back, relax and enjoy the lush landscape as it passes by your window".

"I wonder who the 'other party' were that also received unwanted attention from the unstable Ms Braun", pondered Jasmine.

"There has got to be a reason why she decided to have a go at me, I just can't think what. I have been racking my brains, there has got to be something Cerys".

Cerys shrugged and looked at the stunning views out of her window then at her mobile phone checking for any messages, appearing to avoid eye contact with Jasmine.

"No idea, just put it down to her having some major issues, forget about it now. She's in custody and hopefully she will get the help she needs now."

"Hmm", Jasmine replied, not really understanding why Cerys had been so cool and calm about it. Normally she would have been shouting, demanding that the woman should be tortured, but somehow she seemed a bit distant, but she hadn't been her wild and outrageous self for a while now.

Perhaps it was her Police training, the way they are taught to keep calm in the most stressful situations, she thought, whilst fidgeting on the seat, gripping on as they went around the curves on the road to Hana, the town they were heading for.

"We will stop at Keanae Valley Lookout and Waianapanapa State Park that provide grand views of the ocean and surrounding hills. You'll see Wailua Falls, Puuohokomoa Falls, Waikani Falls and the Ohea Stream and Pools, fascinating natural elements that add to the serenity of the landscape. You will also pass Hookipa Beach, famous for its great windsurfing".

Ted again announced proudly over his speaker. It could be heard in his voice that he was extremely proud of the beautiful views, amazing scenery and serenity that he lived amongst and was part of him.

"Easy for you to say", shouted loudly one of the three ladies, in a brash New York accent.

After many, many clicks of the camera, whoops of the views, gasps of the sights, the group headed off to Hana.

Hana was rural, sleepy but charming.

Once they had arrived, the tour guide gave them time to explore and have lunch.

The girls found a Thai restaurant that looked quite nice and it was called, "Nutcharee's Authentic Thai food". The atmosphere was very friendly, the food smelt delicious.

Jasmine ate the chicken pumpkin curry and Cerys ate the Thai Beef salad.

"Gawd this has to be the tastiest meal I've had since we've been here, how's yours?" Jasmine asked Cerys as she slurped her Thai iced tea after swallowing a very large mouthful of her curry.

"It's really lovely but I'm quite full and bloated", replied Cerys.

"You've have only had a couple of mouthfuls, it's not like you not to finish every morsel on your plate is it love?" joked Jasmine.

"It's just so filling, but gorgeous", replied Cerys.

After their lunch they met the rest of the group and Ted the tour guide, all exchanged stories and experiences of where they ate and headed off to the Tedeschi Winery to sample a few varieties of wine.

After a short, breath taking drive, the winery grounds could be seen sheltered by a magnificent Camphor tree. The group chattered away, tasted a variety of wines made from pineapple, grape and raspberry. The tour and the tasting lasted thirty minutes and the girls had managed to taste everything. The three sixty something ladies and the girls were the only ones that tasted all of the different varieties of wine and all seemed a little merry after the process.

The group landed back in Oahu safely, they waved to each other as they all made their way to their hotel transportation area, after the young Japanese man took a group photo of them all, with his partner in the middle, even the clingy couple seemed to loosen up a bit and shook everyone's hands as they left.

"Aw that was truly amaze-balls wasn't it", said Jasmine as she skipped towards the taxi beaming and full of life.
"I hope heaven looks like Maui and Oahu, that's if I'm allowed in", muttered Cerys in a sombre tone as she looked up to the pale blue sky.
The girls were quiet in the taxi back to their hotel, thinking about their trip.
"Fancy a swim in the pool?" asked Jasmine as she dropped her bag with thud on the floor of their hotel suite.
"I am really tired babes, do you mind if I just hit the sack, feel really wiped out", yawned Cerys.
"You do look a bit peaky, probably all that fresh air and wine. Go on, off to bed with you, sleep well and see you tomorrow. I'm going for a quick dip, won't be long", said Jasmine and she blew a kiss to her sleepy friend.
"Yea nighty night babes", Cerys mumbled as she stripped down to her undies, climbed under her duvet and dozed off as soon as her head hit the pillow.
Jasmine donned her bikini and tied a towel around her waist.
The main pool and hot tubs were surrounded with ocean views, tropical flowers and swaying palm trees.

Two hot tub were located in the main pool area, one of each end of the pool.

After a quick swim in the cool water of the pool, Jasmine returned back to the hotel suite. She still felt quite unnerved about her attack and felt uneasy on her own.

It had never bothered her being on her own before. She was used to going out to restaurants and going to the cinema on her own back home since her divorce, but in a different country and since the "second incident", she felt as though her confidence had taken a knock yet again.

She showered and changed into her oversized t-shirt and sat watching the sunset from her hotel suite window with a glass of pineapple wine from one of the bottles the girls had bought from the winery shop in Maui.

Cerys slept soundly except for the occasional moan and fart that she accidentally let slip, Jasmine almost choking on her wine when she did, desperately trying not to wake her with stifled laughter.

She checked her mobile and saw a few text messages from her family and friends back home, saying hope she was having a great time, all was fine with them etc.

She started to text them back when she heard Cerys' phone start to buzz. She had left it on the coffee table.

"Hmm..... wonder who that is", thought Jasmine.

She picked it up to check but whoever it was rang off, but the screen on the phone said,

"Missed call from L"

"How strange", thought Jasmine, she knew it wasn't Steph Cerys' life-partner and lover as she was listed as "wife" in her contact list.

"Will ask her about that tomorrow", she thought.

She flicked through the channels of the TV that was in the lounge, stopping on a low budget film called,

"Franken- hooker". It was about a medical student who set out to recreate his decapitated fiancée' by building her a new body made of Manhattan street hookers!

"What a load of ….." words failed her as she switched off the TV and drained the last drop of wine from her glass and headed off to bed.

Chapter 15

"How about we use our complimentary tickets for the Luau tomorrow?" asked Cerys as she stuck her fork into her omelette at breakfast.

"Yeah, good idea, before the weather breaks, it's supposed to rain for a few days later this week, just as we are going home", answered Jasmine as she sipped her orange juice.

"Oh yes, who is 'L' by the way?" quizzed Jasmine as she buttered a slice of toast

"Who? What do you mean?" asked Cerys shiftily.

"You had a missed call from someone called 'L' last night when you were asleep. I went to answer your phone but it rang off before I managed to pick it up".

"Ummm, dunno, oooh yes I do", said Cerys hesitantly.

"It's one of the boys, you know, Luke from work on the Search Team, we have two days training when I go back to work. I'll check my messages after. Don't want to think about work yet".

"No me neither. Haven't missed the constant questions and queries of confused and irresponsible people saying, what it is; she said, I said, he said they said; I've lost my wallet, it had three hundred pounds inside it and I am on benefits, I need a lost property number so the social will give a crisis loan. Lying bastards most of them. The majority of them are junkies or drunks, very few are real, yet if you or I or some little old lady lost a purse we would get nothing. We couldn't go to the social could we? Oh no the honest, hardworking tax payer gets diddly squat. I know I shouldn't judge in my job, but I can't help it", ranted Jasmine as she bit into her toast with force.

"I know babes", said Cerys as she put her hand on of Jasmine's as she rested it on the table.

"There ain't nothing we can do about it so no point in letting it get to you. Don't think about work now. Right, let's go and book our places for the Luau shall we?"

They made their bookings for the Luau for the following evening then spent the rest of the day sun bathing on the beach and watching the surfers, sipping cocktails, people watching, sending text messages and silly photos of each other to friends and loved ones back home. They laughed until they almost peed themselves.

"Ahh, what another great day to add to our memories", sighed Cerys as they made their way back to the hotel room. "Shall we go on a mini hike tomorrow? Really feel like having a bit of exercise. I've seen a trail map for the Waimea Falls Park on reception. The trails is on quite a flat road and is surrounded by clean botanical gardens, there is also a fifty foot waterfall there".

"Oh sounds amazing, yeah let's do that, will be a great opportunity to take some more photographs", replied Jasmine in excitement.

"Glad we stayed now?" Cerys asked.

"Of course I am.....sorry about my outburst the other day when I started stuffing my suitcase with clothes....some of them were yours by the way", chuckled Jasmine.

Cerys was awake early the following morning. She checked on Jasmine who was quietly snoring, hair covering her face and leg hanging out of her bed.

She swallowed down two tablets with a mug of coffee that she made from the complimentary coffee pot that was in her room.

She watched the sunrise into a beautiful orange glow. She checked her messages on her mobile phone.

"Hi Cerys, let me know when we can meet again. Got a few reunion photo shoots to do but can make it any evening. Call me or text me with details. Take Care, L".

Cerys replied with a text message, grinning as she sipped her coffee.

The hike was exquisite. They took photos of the lush green plants, the vibrant colours of the oversized tropical plants, flowers, the incredible waterfall and botanical gardens.

"Pure paradise", Jasmine purred as they hiked back to their resort with small backpacks slung over their shoulders.

Both had caught the sun over the last few days and they both had a healthy glow about them. Cerys still looked tired and had small dark circles under her eyes which she disguised with concealer. Jasmine had noticed but put it down to Cerys' reason for taking tablets the other day, period pain, so didn't mention it.

As they were getting ready for the Luau back at the hotel, Cerys cracked open another bottle of sparkling wine that they had put in their cooler.

"Do you realise that we have drank alcohol every day since we left Cardiff airport?" exclaimed Jasmine as she was carefully applying her mascara, stopping occasionally for a quick sip of bubbly.

She sang 'Rehab' by Amy Winehouse and Cerys sang back singing into her hairbrush and dancing with her hand in the air.

Jasmine wore her pale blue, low cut back maxi dress that she wore for one night they were in LA. She had a thin matching shawl to drape over shoulders as the air was becoming a lot cooler in the evenings.

Her hair flowed loosely over her shoulders. She stood in the lounge of the suite applying a very pale, natural coloured plumping lipstick to her lips in her compact mirror, wondering if it would plump her cheeks if she applied it there. She decided against that in case it made her look like a squirrel hoarding its nuts for winter. She saw a glimpse of Cerys in the mirror behind her, shoving tablets in her mouth quickly, trying not to be noticed by her friend.

Jasmine didn't say anything but still felt a little concerned. She was sure her friend would tell her if there was anything to worry about.

Cerys wore her white skinny jeans, which looked a little loose on her backside, and a tight fitted short sleeved black top. Her hair was scooped back into a ponytail.

"No dipping our toes in the ocean this time", laughed Jasmine as they climbed into their taxi to go to the Paradise Cove Luau, part two!

"Too right, I am staying at the bar", replied Cerys as she pushed her friend's backside into the back seat.

Chapter 16

The familiar sound of ukuleles echoed in the air, the smell of the roast and the food being cooked was mouth-watering as the girls made their way to the luau. They were given sweet smelling fresh flower leis along with their complimentary Mai Tai cocktails.

"Aloha, Aloha", could be heard everywhere as the guests were greeted by the staff. The air was cool with a delicate breeze, the lush palms swayed gently as the waves could be heard in the distance breaking onto the beach. The lit torches flickered furiously with every passing flurry of air.

There were lots of groups of people laughing and sharing stories amongst themselves and the waiters, staff and entertainers were busy mingling.

"Aloha, welcome back ladies, how is your foot ma'am?" said a familiar voice as a hand touched Cerys' shoulder.

It was Koka, the kind waiter that looked after Cerys when she squashed a jelly fish last time.

After they exchanged pleasantries and 'thank yous' and the 'see you laters' and were told to stay away from the ocean with a pointed wagging finger, Cery's took hold of Jasmine's hand to find a table. She passed loads of empty tables and Jasmine kept calling out, in between sips and mostly gulps of her cocktail as it sloshed around the glass,

"Here, or how about there, hey where are we going, I'm not sitting on the performance stage".

Cerys didn't stop until she reached a table that was almost full, with just two seats remaining. Jasmine came to a sudden stand still behind her with a Mai Tai moustache that she was suddenly wearing. It had sloshed back up the glass and onto her top lip when they promptly stopped walking.

"Well hello, guess who", sang Cerys coquettishly as she sat down.

Jasmine just stood there, stunned, embarrassed, flushed licking and wiping her top lip.

Cerys patted the chair next to her gesturing for Jasmine to sit down.

"Well well well, hello ladies, you finally made it...... together...at last".

It was Joe, the guy they had met on the beach and were supposed to meet on the night of 'the second incident'. Silence fell amongst the other people sitting at the table as they all turned to face the girls, followed by a loud,

"Hello ladies", as if they were expecting them too.

Joe got up to kiss Cerys on the back of her hand and pulled the chair out for Jasmine to sit down, also kissing her on her hand, whilst she stared hard at Cerys and muttered through tight lips,

"Why didn't you tell me we were meeting.....others?",

Cerys shrugged, winked and clinked her cocktail glass against Jasmine's.

There was a mixture of men and women at the table, but mostly men. They all knew each other and talked loudly with each other and included the banter and chatter with another table that was next to them and also full of people. There was a mixture of North American and British accents bellowing out around the table. It was too noisy for the girls to talk to all of the group around the table and a little dark as they only had one torch lit nearby and two small candles on the table. Jasmine examined the faces of the group, thinking that she knew some of them from somewhere, but couldn't place where after thinking long and hard.

Dylan and Rick were sat next to Jasmine, and Cerys was sat next to Joe. They chatted politely whilst they ate and talked about their holiday. Jasmine apologized for not meeting up after the Halloween parade and explained about the "incident", which they seemed to already know about, somehow.

The drink flowed, Cerys became louder and Jasmine more relaxed.

The glorious entertainment had begun. Fire Poi dancing, knife dancing, (which Jasmine could only watch with her hands covering her eyes, only peeping every now and then between her fingers), and Polynesian dancing which included audience participation, which Cerys volunteered herself for. She, along with other volunteers, had to put on a coconut bra and grass skirt and hula dance to a beating drum. It became faster and faster and those who couldn't keep up with the drum beat and rhythm were called off the stage. Cerys and one other woman, who was a lot shorter than her, were left on the stage, as the others failed, one by one to keep up, shaking and jiggling their hips and backside as if their lives depended on it.

The group at the table, and Jasmine, heckled and whistled as the last set of drum beats began. They started slowly then sped up with force, Cerys and the other short woman blasted it out for the final time until the compere shouted it was a tie. He could see in their eyes the determination and that neither were going to give up, and they would be there all night if he hadn't called it.

Everyone clapped loudly and hoorayed as the women were presented with coconut trophies and a bottle of champagne each. Both were exhausted. Still wearing her coconut bra and grass skirt Cerys popped the cork of the champagne as she headed back towards her friend and the group at the table. Everyone on the table stood up and clapped for her as she took a bow and took a swig of the champagne fizz that had exploded out of the top, and collapsed on her chair.

"That was amazing", Jasmine said as she hugged her friend tightly.

"I've had it, that almost finished me off and my boobs are really sore from banging away in this bra", she replied as she passed the bottle to Jasmine and undid the coconut lingerie. It was now hanging loosely around her neck and every time she moved they banged together making the sound of horses' hooves clacking on the ground. Everyone was quite amused by that.

"Anyone want champagne?" Jasmine offered, but everyone declined.

As the group drank and chattered away a band started to play on the stage. The compere welcomed everyone and called for any song requests as the band started playing, "Dance the night way", by the Mavericks, softly in the background. Some to the group including Dylan, Joe and Rick got up to go to the bar.

"Off to get some jugs of beer ladies so we can compare who are the best drinkers, Brits or Americans". Cerys put her coconut bra on the table,

"We are Welsh-British, if you don't mind.....you will never be able to beat us", laughed Cerys, "only the

Scots can do that", and then whispered to Jasmine that she needed the loo after all that jiggling about and to make room for the beer if it was going to be a contest.

Jasmine, sat on her own, poured some of the champagne into her empty cocktail glass and accidentally snorted when the bubbles went up her nose. Looking around to check that no-one had seen her, she dabbed her nose with a napkin.

The MC announced that someone had requested that the band played Michael Buble's song, "I just haven't met you yet".

Couples and small groups started to make their way to the dance area as the band struck the first couple of notes and then started to sing.

Jasmine had kicked her shoes off under the table, she felt so relaxed. She sang along whilst she sipped her champagne and tapped her foot in the sand along with the music whilst watching the singer and the band. She pulled she shawl around her shoulders as the cool, salty breeze had started to pick up.

She felt a hand on her shoulder and before she could turn around she heard a voice that she had heard before. He quoted the saying,

"Never stand when you can sit down and never sit down when you can lie down".

Jasmine turned around quickly before he finished, wondering who it was and where she had heard that quote before.

"Oh...my...Gawwwwd, it's you... is it you? It is you", she pointed whilst her jaw dropped open wide.

As she went to stand up, her chair became caught on her dress and she instantly flipped backwards, legs in the air, her dress fell back to her thighs, partially showing her underwear.

The stranger helped her to her feet but her shawl was tangled around the chair leg and she almost choked as she tried to straighten up.

The stranger was in a state of helpless, uncontrollable laughter as he attempted again to help her.

"Well I've certainly met you now, at last. Like the song I requested?" he asked as he pointed towards the band and as he brushed the grains of sand from Jasmine's dress.

"It's you, Leo from the TV war series, and your character quoted that - sit down, stand up, lay down -Oh my Gawd", she squealed.

"Care to dance?" he asked as he held out his arms to steady her.

Leo held her close as they danced, then he lifted his arm to twirl her in even closer.

She thought he looked so much more handsome in real life than he did on the screen. His hair was short and light brown and very neatly cut. His eyes looked like a greyish blue colour, and his smile made her swoon. He was wearing fitted jeans and a grey t-shirt that outlined the shape of his toned chest. She had so many questions buzzing around in her head but her body took control and none of the questions seem to make sense. Her mouth was dry, chest felt tight, she had an overwhelming fluttering in her stomach that made it difficult to breath for a short while. She giggled like a school girl as he twirled her again.

"I have to sit down", gasped Jasmine as she lost control of her legs. They felt like jelly from the knees down however her inner thighs tingled with excitement. She felt as if her body was made up of different people...like the poor woman in the film, "Frankenhooker".

"Sit down, lay down or stand up?" laughed Leo

As they sat she took a gulp of the rest of the champagne that was in her cocktail glass.

Leo sat next to her, the rest of the group had sat around the table, including Cerys who was sat at the other end. They were all watching intently and smiling broadly. Cerys raised her glass to Jasmine.

The band were now playing, 'Delilah', by Tom Jones which was requested by Cerys.

"Oh my Gawd, this was all a set up wasn't it? How? But why?", she asked with a surprised tone, her tongue sticking to the roof of her mouth, which was very dry through nervousness, and it made a suction noise as she spoke.

Leo, who also seemed quite nervous, took a drink of his beer that one of the group had poured in a glass and passed to him.

"Well, your friend there", pointing to Cerys as he spoke, "she arranged for us to meet. She knew how much of a fan you were and did a lot of research to locate and contact me and found out that the cast and crew from the TV series were meeting here for a reunion and rehearsal, ready for the memorial day that takes place here is December."

Jasmine looked at Cerys who was beaming, all her teeth on display. She had never seen her looking so happy and pleased with herself.

"I thought I recognised some of faces, Joe especially," squealed Jasmine.

"Well cheers all and I am very pleased to meet you, especially you", she grinned as she raised her glass and turned to Leo.

"Do you remember meeting me once before?" he quizzed.

"No of course not…when?" replied Jasmine.

"Cardiff Airport.....do you still have my penny?"

"What penny....?" Jasmine's 'penny' suddenly dropped.

"You...you were that old man....how?"

"We have a team of makeup artists with us and they helped me out", replied Leo as he pointed to the next table. "I thought it be fun to take a look at you close up without you knowing....I like the book marker by the way", he winked.

Jasmine blushed remembering her homemade book marker with a picture of him on it.

"Cerys contacted me when we were at the airport, met me and pointed you out. We had done a reunion with the cast and crew from the other World War II mini-series of "Band of Brothers" in England and then some of us arranged to fly on to Hawaii from Cardiff, once Cerys and I had made the arrangements"

"Well, thank you,.. thank you so much for doing this for me.....I don't know what to say", Jasmine replied embarrassed by the attention.

"It has been great fun, we've all enjoyed getting involved with all the secrecy and sneaking around, but it's Cerys you have to thank, she has done all the arranging. She arranged your vacation to fit in around us so all this could be possible."

"Thank yoooou", Jasmine mouthed to Cerys who in turn blew her a kiss back.

"Did you enjoy your champagne on the plane over, and the jug of beer at your first attempt at a Luau?"

"You?" asked Jasmine

He winked again.

"I tried to meet up with you then but your friend there decided to murder a jelly fish", he laughed.

"The stranger who went for help...you?"

He nodded.

"Me and some of the other guys also saw you on the beach one day, nice bikini by the way, and Joe, Dylan and Rick decided to have a closer look, then between them and Cerys they plotted to meet up at Lei Lei's bar after the Halloween Parade. How are you by the way? We all searched for you when you didn't show up. When you rang Cerys to say you had been attacked and were back at your hotel, we went back with Cerys to check on you but you were out for the count by the time we got there. Cerys said you had four blow jobs and Eminem was with you". Leo laughed. "Lucky Eminem I say".

"I must have looked a right state", blushed Jasmine as she bit her lip, "and blow jobs are cocktails, and M and M are Max and Mia, a couple from Cardiff who are staying at our resort".

"I didn't see you, as Cerys said you were sleeping but I bet you still looked beautiful", grinned Leo as he brushed her hair away from her face with his fingers.

"Talking about blow jobs already are we, and you've only just officially met", said Cerys loudly as she pulled up a chair and joined the couple.

"Cheers", the three said as they clinked their glass.

Chapter 17

Cerys had gone onto bed when they got back to the resort. The rest of the group, who were staying at the same resort in the lavish beach cottages on the west shore of the scenic Turtle Bay, also said goodnight as they left Jasmine and Leo walking along the beach. They walked and talked for what seemed like hours, telling each other about their lives and jobs and families.

"So, do you have a girlfriend or partner back home in Canada?" asked Jasmine shyly.

"No, I'm single", Leo sighed. "It's difficult to keep a relationship going as I travel quite a lot with my acting jobs. I travel between Los Angeles and Canada several times a year. How about you, do you have a 'Mister Jasmine' back home?"

"No, I'm divorced, my ex swapped me for a younger model", Jasmine laughed nervously.

"What an idiot. So... we are both singletons just floating along in life. Would you ever want to get married again?"

"I do I do…yes Leo I will marry you"...said Jasmine jokingly as she pushed him. He shook his head and pushed her back gently.

"Hmmm... not sure, maybe if Mr Right came along, who knows. How about you?" she replied.

"Maybe, one day, it's not for me right now because of work commitments. It would be nice to grow old with someone though. We'll see."

"Make sure you invite me to you wedding then", laughed Jasmine.

Leo nudged her, "You are on the top of my guest list".

The sun began to rise, the sky was dark purple with slithers of orange poking through. Clouds began to gather and random drops of rain began to fall.

"We had better take shelter…and maybe get some shut eye…I didn't realise we had been chatting for so long. I've really enjoyed your company", said Leo.

The heavens opened at the rain began to fall hard and fast as Leo took hold off Jasmine's hand as they ran back to her hotel suite.

They were soaked by the time they arrived at her door. Her dress was soaked through and her breasts and erect nipples and knickers were on display for all to see. She tried to wrap her shawl around her to hide her embarrassment but Leo stopped her.

"Don't…. you look so beautiful", he said as he examined her body hungrily. He looked around to see if there was anyone around. He pushed her hair from her face with both hands. They stared into each other's eyes, Jasmine's heart was racing, her legs felt shaky, her inner thighs and breasts started to tingle as he drew her chin towards him with one finger. Every pleasure point in her body had ignited. He kissed her gently, then pulled away, still staring into her eyes, Jasmine returned the kiss, this time neither pulled away. Leo took hold of her tightly in his arms and Jasmine caressed his toned back through his wet t-shirt as she wrapped her arms around him. Their tongues were entwined, twisting and twirling inside each other's mouths. Leo pushed her up against the door, she could feel his excitement pressing up against her through his wet jeans and her wet dress.

He pressed harder and harder, Jasmine thought she was going to explode as he tenderly stroked her nipple with the palm of his hand. She moaned with pleasure as he pushed his tongue deep into her mouth.

"What the hell is going on...oops...sorry" said Cerys as she opened the door to the hotel suite and both fell through with force, landing on the floor, with Leo laying on top of Jasmine and with one hand on her breast

Cerys kept saying sorry as she hurried off back to her bed.

Leo stood up and pulled Jasmine up with both of his hands, both blushing with embarrassment.

"You can stay if you want to Leo, I'll stick my headphones in so I can't hear anything", shouted Cerys.

"I'd better go", he shouted back, whilst staring at Jasmine.

"Thank you for a wonderful evening Jas. Um would you like to come to dinner with me tonight?" he asked.

"Yes she would", shouted Cerys.

"I would love to", replied Jasmine, giggling.

"I'll call you later then. Get some sleep", he whispered as he kissed her softly on the lips and tapped her gently on the nose with his finger, before leaving.

Jasmine ran into Cerys bedroom and jumped on her bed like an excited child on Christmas morning.

"Get off, you're wet", screamed Cerys.

"Too right I am", said Jasmine with a naughty glint in her eye.

"Get changed and tell me all about it", tutted Cerys.

Jasmine dried herself off and changed into her oversized t-shirt and climbed into bed with Cerys.

"Thank you mate...so much. You are the most amazing friend. You must have been organising this for months"

"Aw shucks, I've loved every bloody minute of it and it was worth it all the secret phone calls, arrangements, sneaking around just to see your face when you first met.... and when I opened the door to find you both snogging, it made my heart melt", Cerys said with a tear in her eyes.

Cerys yawned and rolled over on to her back after they had been talking for a while.

"Sleep now babes, talk more later okay".

Jasmine couldn't sleep, she had a permanent grin on her face as she went over in her mind the events of the evening and morning.

She finally drifted off, still grinning as she imagined what could have happened if Cerys hadn't opened the door.

"Mmmmm" she mumbled to herself.

Chapter 18

The rain had stopped when the girls finally woke up, which was mid-morning. Jasmine still grinning as they both drank coffee in Cery's bed.

"Are you sure you don't mind me going to dinner with Leo this evening? I feel awful leaving you", said Jasmine

"Oh my Gawd, I want you to go, you deserve this so much. I have been chatting to him on the phone, via Skype for the last two months and he has been dying to meet you, besides it would be nice to have a bit of me time, you know what I mean", winked Cerys.

Jasmine hopped out of bed and stretched out her arms, yawned loudly then bent forward to stretch out her hamstrings before heading to the bathroom to shower. She sang Kylie's song

"I just can't get you out of my head", as she scrubbed her skin with the loofah, shaved her legs, under her arms and tidied her bikini line...just in case.

"So, do you think you will be staying out tonight then?" asked Cerys as Jasmine was moisturising her legs.

A sudden rush of fear flushed through Jasmine's body. She began to worry that if she did sleep with Leo, that would be it, no more wondering, lusting, dreaming or imagining and he probably wouldn't want to see her again afterwards. Then she worried that she wouldn't see him again anyway as she lived in Wales and he lived just over three thousand miles away in Canada, and would pine for him even more. So, she decided that they would have a lovely evening, maybe have a little kiss but that would be it, there was no point in taking it any further.

"Nope, just dinner, nothing else", replied Jasmine dismissively.

"What, there is definitely chemistry between you, go for it, enjoy it, we get one shot of this life, go for it if you really want it, there's no shame, life is for living babes and what's the saying, 'better to have fucked Leo and lost than never to have fucked him at all", laughed Cerys.

"It's better to have loved and lost than never to have loved at all and there may be chemistry between us but there will be a bloody big ocean between us as well when we scuttle back off home to reality. I can't, it wouldn't be fair", shrugged Jasmine

"Fair- schmare? What's fair anymore? You like him and he likes you...I saw how excited he was when he fell through the door last night, could have hung my washing on him. Do me a favour though, take these just in case?" Cerys handed Jasmine a box of condoms. "You don't want to be a mother again at your age...or catch anything".

"I won't need them....... maybe one…just in case, but I won't need it", replied Jasmine shaking her head but at the same time stuffing a couple of condoms in her bag.

They spent the warm, sunny afternoon on Segways that they hired from the hotel, embarking on an adventure exploring Turtle Bay's exotic trails. Both wearing denim cut off shorts and vest tops, with support bras, because of the wobble factor, and cycle helmets, they headed off, screaming and laughing as they learned how to manoeuvre their two wheeled devices. Their tour guide and instructor, Dom, was great fun. He must have been about twenty years old, about six foot ten, with feet the size of water skis, wearing long shorts and a Segway instructor t-shirt, in case they didn't know which one was the instructor. He zipped away in front of them with confidence and ease, followed by Cerys, but Jasmine lagged behind.

"Come on Miss Daisy, be brave, put some welly into it girlie", yelled Cerys.

Jasmine, not the most confident and a bit of a technophobe gritted her teeth and attempted to go faster to catch up.

The views along the various trails were out of this world. Dom took them to secluded shores where the water was so clear it was like glass, to show them sea turtles and Hawaiian monk seals that were basking in the sun. They took an umpteen amount of photographs before heading off further along the trail to see a World War II airstrip and a bunker site. The airstrip, called the Kahuku Army Airfield, was used for training in the war. It was no longer in use and now the Turtle Bay golf course absorbed two of the runways. Very little evidence of Kahuku's World War II fortifications remained except one bunker site that keeps its past military secrets. The entrance to the bunker was buried in sand leaving only two concrete structures exposed.

"This bunker entrance was featured in the films Pearl Harbour and Jurassic Park", exclaimed Dom as he whizzed off ahead of the girls.

"Leo would love all this army history", mused Jasmine, due to his acting role as an Army Captain, whilst daydreaming about her forthcoming dinner date.

As they headed back they could see the seven mile stretch of beautiful white sand, sloping coastal shelves with epic waves crashing on to them up to about five stories high and the incredible natural beauty that surrounded them.

"Shangri-La", announced Dom as they stopped to admire the breath taking spectacle.

"That was amazing, thanks Dom". Cerys said graciously as their Segways came to a standstill at the resort's activity centre, Jasmine arriving a short time after.

"Phew that was brilliant, thanks mate", said Jasmine, slightly breathless, "but my bum and back are aching", she winced.

"It can take a while to learn how to balance and manoeuvre around on them but some take to it like a duck to water". Dom nodded at Cerys who was looking quite proud of herself.

The girls made their way to the Lobby Lounge at the resort to treat themselves to a well-earned cocktail. Cerys had a "Skinny Rita", which was a mixture of tequila, orange liqueur, lime juice, agave nectar and coconut water and Jasmine ordered a "Kula Cooler", to cool her down. Her cocktail was filled with VeeV acai spirit, strawberry and fresh lime sour.

Their glasses were huge. They guzzled and giggled and talked about the forthcoming evening.

"I am so excited for you, my 'liddle' girlie going on a date with a movie star", said Cerys as she tickled her friend under the chin.

Jasmine almost choked as she guzzled her drink back a bit too quickly through her straw.

"I don't think he's a movie star," she laughed.

"Let's get you ready, come on", Cerys slurped the remainder of her cocktail and held out her hand to

Jasmine. They waved at the bar tender as they headed off to their suite.

Jasmine headed for the shower whilst Cerys rooted around her wardrobe for something for her to wear. She pulled out a sleeveless, red cotton, knee length dress that was fitted at the waist and hips and a dropped neckline. She had a pair of wedged, red matching sandals to go with it.

"I think that'll be too tight for me", said Jasmine as she emerged from the shower with a big white fluffy towel wrapped around her.

"You're so much thinner than I am".

She dried herself with the towel, moisturised her legs again so they looked supermodel shiny and put on the sexiest knickers and bra she could find.

"Wuu -woo, are you sure you are straight?" whistled Cerys as she jokingly licked her lips.

"Sorry, meat and two veg only for me", laughed Jasmine

"Nothing wrong with a bit of fish", Cerys replied

"Ewww! Too far", Jasmine grimaced.

The dress fitted perfectly although it was a little tight on her backside.

"You have a skinny arse missy", exclaimed Jasmine

"Does mine look like a sumo wrestler's?" she asked as she attempted to sit down, trying not to rip it, but it was surprisingly quite giving".

"You look as sexy as fuck, now put your slap on and I'll do your hair", replied Cerys.

The shoes were slightly too big so Jasmine wore a pair of black sling-backs that she had packed. Cerys had styled her hair like a 1950's film star. Her dark, soft, loose, flowing feminine curls cascaded over her shoulders. Her makeup was subtle and natural. She didn't need much as her skin was beautifully tanned.

"Perfect", exclaimed Cerys as there was a knock at the door.

"Wow", said Leo as Jasmine opened the door and he stepped inside the suite, kissing her lightly on the lips. Jasmine tingled again from every naughty place on her body.

They headed off for dinner arm in arm as Cerys waved them off.

"Have a good time y'all, and take care of my girl", she shouted after them.

"See ya later mam", replied Jasmine sarcastically.

Cerys shut the door and took a deep breath and clutched her stomach. She took a couple of tablets, and later ordered a pizza and small bottle of wine from room service then went to bed, feeling very tired, drained, aching from head to toe, (which she declined to mention to Jasmine), but very pleased with herself that she had finally given her best mate a piece of happiness.

Chapter 19

Leo, dressed in a light blue, short sleeved shirt and tight, navy cargo trousers that extenuated his tight but muscular backside, led Jasmine a short distance to a bar and restaurant called 'The Surfer' which was on the resort. Both were quite nervous after the night before and made small talk as they walked.

He smelt like fresh, clean cotton as he stood close behind and pulled her chair out for her to sit down. Her heart was beating so fast she was sure he could hear it.

"I know I've said this a few times on the way but you look gorgeous", exclaimed Leo as he took hold of Jasmine's hand and kissed it.

"You look pretty damn good too", giggled Jasmine.

"Can I get you a drink, whilst you look at the menu?" asked the waiter who just appeared from nowhere.

"Bottle of house red okay?" Leo asked Jasmine. She nodded excitedly.

"Well, this is my last night in this beautiful place, I fly back to Canada tomorrow afternoon", said Leo sadly.

"I know, we have to fly back home the day after tomorrow, to cold, dark, wet Wales too. We've had the best time, best holiday, and........you have made it, well....amaze-balls", remarked Jasmine.

"Ha haaa...Amaze-balls? I've never heard of that before but I like it and will borrow that if you don't mind", laughed Leo.

They ordered their meals of Hawaiian smoked pork with caramelized Maui onions and shitake mushrooms and a classic Caesar salad. As they ate and talked a Hawaiian band played, "Somewhere over the Rainbow/It's a wonderful world" in the style of the musician Israel K, on the stage that was located in the bar.

"The Surfer bar stage is a well-known stage for Hawaiian musicianship, which shows an unlikely mash up of traditional Hawaiian, modern rock, hip hop and reggae,", remarked the waiter as he handed each table little comment cards as he walked passed.

"You have to come to Canada for a holiday and I will come visit you in Wales right?" said Leo as he topped up their glasses and placed the comment cards to one side.

"Love to, but it's a lot of money and you will forget all about me as soon as you get back home anyway.....all those gorgeous film starry types you knock around with will make your time with me a distant memory.....but...if ever you do visit the UK, you must look me up though", replied Jasmine, trying to be jolly but deep inside she felt extremely sad.

"I will NEVER forget you and we WILL meet again. I want to see you again. I didn't know what to expect before I met you properly, 'but you had me' when you ended upside down when your chair flipped back at the Luau." He pulled her face towards his and kissed her on the cheek.

"We'll meet again, don't know where don't when, but I know we'll meet again some sunny day", sang Jasmine.

"Did anyone tell you that you have a terrible singing voice?" laughed Leo as Jasmine flipped his arm.

"Hey you two, get a room", could be heard from the doorway. It was a couple of Leo's group that he had travelled with him for the reunion. They waved and headed towards the bar.

"Won't be long" said Leo as he stood up, scooped the last morsel of his meal into his mouth, and went to the bar to speak to them.

"Oi, where are you going, not leaving me to pay the bill I hope?", Jasmine called after him. He turned around and winked then spoke to his friends and the bar tender. "Charming", she muttered to herself. They disappeared behind the bar, then reappeared on the stage.

"What the......" thought Jasmine, as she placed her knife and fork down on her plate.

Leo and his friends were on the stage. They spoke to the band and then music started to play.

"Oh shit, they're going to sing", Jasmine thought as she looked around the now crowded bar and restaurant area. She rested her elbows on the table and covered her face with embarrassment as the group sang to her and walked towards her, Leo was lead vocals and stood right in front of her as he sang Otis Redding's' "Try a little tenderness". Leo blasted out the chorus in a gravelly and soulful rasp.

Everyone stood up and clapped as Leo and the group took a bow. He handed the microphone back to the band on the stage, shook his friend's hands and headed back to Jasmine. His friend's went back to the bar, blowing kisses as they went.

Jasmine flung her arms around Leo.

"That was brilliant. Loved it, a proper Tom Cruise, Top Gun moment", she laughed then kissed him passionately on the lips.

"More wine?" he asked, looking a little flushed and pulling her chair closer to his.

"Mmm yes please", replied Jasmine, still feeling awestruck from what had just happened, the song and the kiss.

The waiter brought over another bottle and topped up their glasses as Leo kissed Jasmine's neck then the back of her hand. She started to feel quite hot and tingly all over.

"So what's you guilty pleasure", Leo whispered in her ear.

"Glee", replied Jasmine.

Leo almost spat his wine out with laughter

"Really? That show with the kids that sing...really?" he laughed.

"What else?" he dared to ask.

"Chocolate, wine, old movies, Branston pickle, I love having my neck and back stroked gently...and right now...you". She replied, looking away shyly.

"What's Branston...no don't answer", he laughed.

"What's yours?" Jasmine asked

"I love listening to BB King, obviously love to splendour in the taste of liquor and history of the twentieth century military, I like having my neck and back stroked as well....and I like you too", he replied and kissed her on the nose quickly.

"What is your favourite word?" purred Jasmine

"Okay so we are doing the 'Bouillon De Culture', Pivots questionnaire from James Lipton's Inside the

Actors studio are we?" he remarked with a smirk and reeled off his answers without Jasmine asking him.

"Yes, is my favourite word.....least favourite is No. Life turns me on and negativity turns me off. My favourite curse word is Fuck as is covers all aspects, my least is the 'C' word, I won't say it in your presence. Umm... my favourite sound is laughter, least favourite is the sound of crying and sadness. The other profession other than my own I would like to have attempted is hmm…maybe the military. I would not like to have done politics and if Heaven exists, I would like God to say when I arrive at the Pearly Gates....come on in, it's party time and there are loads of people you have been 'dying'...excuse the pun...to meet....taa-dah...your turn"

"Okay, my favourite word is serendipity, my least is the 'N' word which I detest, positivity turns me on and hate and negativity turn me off too, my favourite curse word is bollocks....ooh and bugger.. and my least is the same as yours, the 'C' word. My favourite sound is the sound of summer, children playing and laughing, lawnmowers mowing, bees buzzing but my least favourite sound is sirens as you know someone, somewhere needs help. The other profession other than my own would be a mid-wife/nurse or zoo keeper, can't decide, I would not like to have gone into politics either, and if Heaven exists, I would like God to say when I arrive at the Pearly Gates, welcome Jasmine, remember what happens on earth stays on earth now go and meet Elvis and Marilyn", Jasmine chuckled.

"Nice one", grinned Leo as he clinked Jasmine's glass with his.

"Shall we drink up and go for a stroll on the beach?"

"I need to powder my nose first, won't be long", Jasmine whispered, feeling very excited and giddy about having Leo all to herself, away from the now over packed bar.

Leo look concerned and lowered his eyebrows

"No, nooooo, not like that.... I'm not a coke head...I mean use the loo, and re-apply face powder to my nose... it's an expression", said Jasmine trying to redeem herself, Leo laughed as she over pronounced her wiggle as she walked away from the table almost slipping off her heels. She could feel his eyes following her.

As Jasmine walked into a cubicle and shut the door, in the ladies loos, she sang to herself happily and feeling slightly tipsy

"I should be so lucky lucky lucky lucky, I should be so lucky in luuurve".

She heard someone walking into the Ladies loo, sounded like they had flip flops on, and they turned a tap on, so she stopped singing promptly. She had finished peeing and used the flush and unlocked the cubicle door. She pushed the door but it appeared to be jammed. She pushed it again harder this time, but it still wouldn't budge.

"Hello, Hello can anyone hear me, I'm stuck, hello", she yelled out.

No-one answered.

"Shit, shit", Jasmine scrambled around in her handbag for her phone but as she did she heard the entrance door open again.

"Hello?...Help...I'm stuck"

"Okay, hold on, there seems to be something jammed in the lock mechanism", said an older lady's voice the other side of the door.

The door suddenly opened and the lady the other side held out a small pocket knife that had been rammed into the lock.

"Are you okay?" asked the lady who was short and round like a cottage loaf. "How on earth did that get in there?" said the lady examining the instrument with her glasses balancing on the end of her nose.

"I have absolutely no idea, but thank you so much", said Jasmine breathlessly and a little unnerved.

"You're welcome Ma'am. Now I shall dispose of this in the trash so it doesn't get in the wrong hands. Have a nice evening", remarked the lady as she threw it in the bin and disappeared into a cubicle.

Jasmine washed her hands quickly, checked her makeup and headed back to Leo, wondering how the hell a small knife ended up there.

As she walked back to the table, she could see a woman facing the opposite way sat next to Leo.

"Hi", she said, thinking it was one of Leo's group as she sat down and joined them.

Terror, horror and fear crept over her as the female sat next to Leo was Astrid.

"I vucking told you to stay away from Zer Skipper you stupid beech," scowled Astrid.

"Zer Skipper? You are Zer Skipper?" asked Jasmine, confused.

Leo nodded whilst biting his bottom lip nervously.

"It's thee skipper, it's my nick name as I played a Captain in that series", he mumbled.

"I thought they locked you up, how did you get out...I'm calling the police", said Jasmine frantically. She reached for her mobile in her handbag.

"If you call cops zer Skipper's balls vill be on zee floor, put phone away...sstupid. Now, all ov us valk out slowly." she scowled again.

His face was white, all the colour had drained out of his cheeks. He stared hard into Jasmine's eyes and she could see the worry flash across them as they stood up.

Jasmine could see as she moved away from the table that Astrid was holding a steak knife to Leo's crotch which was hidden under her jacket that was slung over her arm.

Jasmine walked slowly in front and Leo and Astrid followed closely behind.

A sudden rush of anger pulsated through Jasmine's body. It devoured her fear and terror. She spun around quickly,

"You are becoming a major pain in the backside love and I don't give a hot monkey's ass if this hurts or not", Jasmine yelled and punched Astrid right in the nose and then in the throat. She fell backwards and dropped the knife just as a troop of police officers flew through the bar door pointing their guns at the mad women. The whole bar went quiet, a few hushed words and mumblings echoed around the room, the music stopped.

Astrid muttered what sounded like German swear words under her breath as the police carted her off.

"Bloede Kuh", and "Dreckige Hure" She mumbled and spat at Jasmine as she was carried passed, luckily she missed.

"Are you both okay", asked the police officer that Jasmine had seen before.

"My hand is bloody sore", Jasmine winced as she rubbed her knuckles.

"How the hell did she escape?" she asked.

"She scaled the wall of the exercise yard at the unit where she was being held, whilst the guard was distracted for a few moments. She is one fit woman. We went to your hotel room as soon as we heard she had escaped and your friend told us you had come here with this gentleman. She won't bother you again, I can assure you of that".

"You said that last time", remarked Jasmine as she checked her phone and noticed that she had loads of missed calls and messages from Cerys. She quickly sent a text to Cerys to reassure her they were fine.

"Sorry again ma'am and sir", said the police officer as he tipped his hat and followed the rest of officers to their cars with Astrid in handcuffs.

The music started up again and the mumbling stopped and everyone returned to what they were doing before the furore.

As the police and their prisoner left, Leo's group of friends rushed over clapping Jasmine's punches and with a bucket of ice for her hand.

"Are you okay Jas?" Leo said as he hugged her tightly.

"Who the hell is that mad bitch to you?" she said pulling away angrily.

"She works in a bar back home. She has become obsessed with me. She hacked my computer and phone and followed me everywhere, from Canada to LA, turning up at parties and she even hung around outside the Emmy awards ceremony. I've told her over and over that I'm not interested and have even taken out an injunction against her."

"Oh, right", said Jasmine listening intently.

"When I heard she had followed me here, I informed the police straight away. She must have seen the messages that Cerys and I exchanged about meeting you when she hacked my phone, and became jealous. Gawd, I'm so sorry Jas", he said as he hugged her again, this time she hugged him back.

"Yep she has been a right pain in the ass, she has scared the shit out of Leo over these last few years", exclaimed one of Leo's friends as he patted him on the back.

"I need some fresh air", Jasmine whispered to Leo with tears in her eyes.

"Goodnight guys, it was wonderful meeting you all, have a safe trip home", she said to Leo's friends.

"Hope to see you again Jas", they shouted as Jasmine hot footed it out of the bar.

Leo spoke to his friend's briefly, he borrowed a pen from the waiter and wrote, "Great food, great music but some scary customers", on the comment card that was on the table, paid the bill, and then chased after Jasmine.

He found her sat on the beach, with her shoes in her one hand, toes buried in the sand, hair blowing wildly and curls tangling in the breeze. She was speaking to Cerys on the phone as she had left Jasmine a message demanding she rang her back.

"I'm fine honestly love," Leo heard her saying as she wiped her tears away.

"Yep he's here and that crazy moo has been carted off again. See you later...love ya babes, night-night".

Leo scooped her up in his arms and cuddled her so hard she couldn't breathe.

"Come back to the beach house, I don't want to let you go, I just love your accent...so cute, so..... strange", he whispered in a soft velvety tone as he pressed his lips against her cheek and then tried to imitate her Welsh accent which resulted in him earning another flip on his arm.

"Stop taking the piss...you.... maple syrup loving.... Mountie". She shouted, desperately trying think of something to call him.

Leo couldn't stop laughing at the weakest, most ridiculous insult he had ever heard!

Chapter 20

As the pair walked towards the beach house where Leo was staying, Jasmine hesitated and came to a stop. Leo, holding her hand tightly, both their arms stretched as he had continued to walk, also stopped.

"What is it?" he asked, as he turned towards her and placed his hands on her waist.

"I don't know what to do", she replied quietly.

"What do you mean Jaz, do what?" he said with a puzzled expression on his face.

"If I sleep with you, it will break my heart as you are jetting back home tomorrow and I will probably never see you again, If I don't sleep with you then I will kick myself and it will break my heart and.....and". Jasmine realised that she had said it out loud, not meaning to. It was supposed to stay in her head. She looked at Leo's face, his eyes were wide open and so was his mouth.

"Shit, shit.....sorry, you weren't meant to hear that".

They both burst out laughing and he held her tightly to his chest.

"You don't have to do anything you don't want to do. I didn't bring you here to have sex with you".

Jasmine was secretly disappointed, Leo continued,

"Well, I mean that wasn't what was on my mind,well it was - still is, but only if it felt right and it was what you wanted as well....I think I'm making a pig's ear out of this aren't I?"

Both laughed nervously, held each other's hands and walked towards the beach house.

As they approached his elegantly appointed beach house, they experienced a vision of imperial yellow and copper accents against a backdrop of azure seas. As Leo opened the door, Jasmine couldn't believe her eyes. Inside she found polished, walnut floors leading to a large, multi-level beach retreat with fifteen foot ceilings and king poster bed. There was a kallista deep soak tub in the bathroom that she had only ever seen in magazines.

"Oh my...this is just....."

"Amaze-balls?" interrupted Leo.

"I was going to say beautiful", laughed Jasmine.

"I love it, I really don't want to leave", said Leo as he manoeuvred Jasmine to the Lanai.

"Beer?" he asked.

"Yes please", answered Jasmine as she sat down at the little wicker garden table and chairs, overlooking the beach and the ocean. The sound of the waves crashing on the shore and the salty breeze made her feel relaxed. She reflected on the evening earlier, frowning at the thought of Astrid escaping and what she would have done to them if she hadn't punched her. She felt Leo's hand gently touch her on shoulder as he sat down beside her, holding two bottles of beer in his hand he placed hers in front of her and took a large swig from his.

"Phew", he said with a sigh.

"What an eventful evening that was, well it has been an eventful vacation really".

"Here's to less scary eventful-nesses in the future", laughed Jasmine nervously as she clinked her bottle against Leo's.

"This sure is a beautiful place", remarked Leo

"Hmmmm", replied Jasmine as she sipped her beer.

There was silence for a while. They kept looking at each other, catching each other's stare and then looking away again. Eventually they broke their hush and began to talk and chatter but both felt slightly awkward. They both fancied the backsides off each other but both were too nervous to make a move after Jasmine's little 'mind outburst' on their walk to the house.

"May I use the loo?" asked Jasmine.

"Of course, go right ahead, I'll get us another beer", said Leo as he pointed to the direction of the bathroom.

"Won't pee long", giggled Jasmine.

Leo rolled his eyes and gave her a wide smile.

Jasmine shut the door of the bathroom and rummaged around in her bag for her phone.

She sent a text to Cerys.

"Dilemma!!!....I want to shag him....not sure if he wants to shag me...Oh I feel like I'm a slut...will he think I'm a slut?...Bugger, bum...help!!!!"

Text from Cerys.

"Oh- my- Gawd, grow up you silly cow...shag him or I will kill you ....or worse.... I will never speak to you again. Smiley face ."

Text from Jasmine.

"I could lie to you and tell you I have shagged him and not shag him."

Text from Cerys.

"Jas, you couldn't lie if your life depended on it. This guy really…I mean REALLY likes you. Just have fun, like I keep saying, you get one shot at this life...no regrets hey…now fuck off and leave me alone...smiley face".

Text from Jasmine.

"I'm fucking off...night night".

There was a knock on the bathroom door.

"Jas, you okay, you haven't escaped out of the window have you?" called Leo.

She opened the door and he handed her a beer

"Eww...were you listening to me pee you pervert?" she laughed.

With that he took the bottle out of her hand and placed it on the wooden cupboard in the room. He kissed her so hard she almost stopped breathing. She kissed him back passionately, touching his chest tenderly with her palms, then slowly moving them down to his hips and thighs. He echoed her movements. She winced with excitement as he softly touched her breasts and then he moved his hands down the contour of her body. She no longer had control over her mind, her body wanted him so badly her inner thighs ached for him. She started to unbutton his shirt but as she did he pulled away, took a deep breath and took her hand. He led her towards the bedroom. He continued to kiss her hard, not taking a breath, kissing her lips then her neck and throat and back to her lips. Their tongues entwined, swirling and twirling inside each other's mouths.

He took off his shirt and Jasmine took off her dress. She unbuttoned his trousers and gently brushed her hands against his extremely hard length.

He breathed heavily as she pulled his trousers down, dropping to her knees and brushing her breast against his thighs as she did. He took hold of her hands and pulled her back to her feet. He kissed her neck and throat and moved his hands around to her back to undo her bra. He slowly pulled it off and kissed her breasts and teased her nipples with his tongue. Jasmine was in ecstasy, she moaned with pleasure as she slowly placed her fingers around the top of his boxers and pulled them down. Her hands caressed his erect manhood. Leo kissed her breasts hard and he moved Jasmine on to the bed. He removed his boxers from around his ankles and then removed Jasmines panties as he kissed her stomach. She felt as if she was going to explode. Her heart was pounding, her breathing was speedy, butterflies tingled in her stomach and she was very wet inside. He kissed hard and licked deep between her thighs. Jasmine groaned in the back of her throat.

Leo pulled himself up and led on top of her, writhing, kissing her and caressing her, he slowly reached for the bedside cabinet drawer and pulled out a small packet.

He sat up, straddling Jasmine, expertly rolled a condom onto his erection, slid back down and....

"Oh my Gaaaaaaawd", yelled Jasmine as he thrust himself deep into her, over and over and over and over again.

He was very gentle with her after. Still laying on top of her, he kissed her lips and stroked her hair and then he rolled onto his back pulling her on to his chest. They lay for a while in each other's arms, she stroking and kissing his chest, he stroking her hair, neck and back and kissing her forehead. Playfully he started to tickle her and she tickled him back. She moved on top of him, sat up and straddled him.

"You are so damn sexy", he said with serious face as he reached up and brushed her cheek with the back of his hand.

For a moment he looked worried and then sad.

For a moment Jasmine had a flash of fear that raged through her body as she examined his expression. Her heart felt heavy.

"Oh Gawd, are you thinking that I'm a slut...I don't do this, this isn't me", Jasmine whimpered with a tear in her eye as she tried to dismount.

"Stop, no", Leo grabbed her wrist and pulled her back down onto him, her inner thighs pressed either side of his hips.

"I just don't want to go home yet. We've only just properly started to get to know each other...and I love spending time with you... and by the way missy", Leo changed the mood to a more light hearted one, sat up, pulled her legs around his waist so that Jasmine was in his lap, continued,

"you are not a slut, I don't do this all the time either, you are so ...."

"Amaze balls?", laughed Jasmine, also feeling more light hearted after his mood had changed...."Actually", she looked down between her thighs, "You do have amazing balls" she giggled. He grinned then kissed her softly on the lips.

Jasmine sighed with relief. She still had very little confidence in herself and always thought the worst, but now she felt relieved.

He pulled her in close and she could feel his excitement rising.

"Hmmmm again?" she whispered sensually in his ear.

He nodded, grinned, eyes narrowed, hips began to move up and down.

She reached across him with one hand and pulled out another little packet from the drawer at the side of the bed. She sat back, he laid back and she ripped the little packet open with her teeth.

"Let me", he said and took the packet from her hand, rolled the condom onto his excitement, threw the packet on the floor, lifted Jasmine onto him. She writhed around on top of him, both moaning with pleasure. She leaned forward and kissed him hard and deep, tongues entwined, hands caressing each other. Leo sat up and pulled her close. They slowed their rhythm, kissed more sensually, he lifted her off, rolled her onto her back and laid on top of her, pushing her thighs open with his. He looked into her eyes and she looked deep into his. They felt as one. He kissed her softly and threw his final thrust deep into her, both moaned and reached their climax at the same time.

They laid side by side, holding hands staring at each other, until sleep finally carried them away. Leo drifted off first. He was snuggled close up to Jasmine's face. She watched him for a while and as she closed her eyes he sleepily muttered,

"I love you Jasmine".

She struggled to keep her eyes open, she wasn't sure if she was dreaming or if he really said it. She couldn't fight it anymore and drifted off as well.

Chapter 21

Jasmine was awoken by something soft stroking her cheek. She turned round to find Leo lying next to her with a single coral coloured, bell shaped flower in his hand. He dabbed her nose with it as she uttered,

"Good morning....mmmmm...I had a flower exactly the same as that on my pillow my hotel in LA".

She sat up suddenly.

"You?" she asked inquisitively.

"Yep", said Leo coyly. "I asked the receptionist to put a flower in your room for me, Gawd I must sound like a right stalker. Me and the guys stayed at the same hotel as you, all arranged by Cerys, we also saw you at Pearl Harbour".

Jasmine grinned like a Cheshire cat.

"Is there ANYTHING else that you haven't told me?" queried Jasmine.

"I don't think so, other than you snore like a chainsaw and break wind like a pack mule when you sleep", he laughed.

"No I don't", screamed Jasmine as she hit him with a pillow.

He grabbed a pillow and hit her back. They chased each other around the room like a dog chasing a cat. Eventually, they both gave up and flopped back on the bed.

"Okay, no wind breaking, but you do snore a little bit", grinned Leo.

"Well you talk in your sleep", replied Jasmine coquettishly.

"Oh yeah, what did I say?" enquired Leo.

Jasmine didn't want to repeat that he had said he loved her.

"I dunno, you mumbled something but I couldn't understand what you were saying".

"Yeah yeah", replied Leo as he pushed her back and laid on top of her.

"Oh no I must have morning breath", said Jasmine as she covered her mouth with her hand.

Leo pulled it away and kissed her tenderly. She kissed him back and before long, he reached for a condom, slipped it on and he was inside her again. He was more warm and affectionate this time, not as rampant as before. They made love until the sun glistened through the window.

There was a knock at the door.

"Skip, are you there bruv?" called a familiar voice.

Leo leapt out of bed and wrapped a towel around his waist before going to the door.

Jasmine could hear several male voices, laughing and talking loudly. She got dressed quickly, tidied her hair and face up in the bathroom and made her way to where all the chatter was coming from.

Leo and a few of the guys he had travelled with were stood chatting on the lanai.

"Well, good morning Miss Jasmine, how are you? Sorry to interrupt, we have to grab Leo for a final meeting with the cast and crew before we head home. Last minute thing.... sorry".

"Hi", replied Jasmine shyly as she stood by the door of the bedroom, feeling slightly embarrassed.

"Oh...of course, no problem, I'll grab my stuff and leave you alone", she said quite disappointed.

"Wait Jas", replied Leo.

"Guys, let me get dressed and then I will meet you at the venue in ten, okay".

Jasmine stayed in the doorway of the bedroom, feeling dejected.

"Okay, see ya in ten buddy", said one of the guys.

"See ya Jas, have a good trip home doll", he shouted, walked out the door followed by the other guys who all high fived Leo as they went.

"I had better let you get ready", said Jasmine gathering her bag and shoes.

"Wait", said Leo as he grabbed her waist and pulled her towards him. She dropped her bag and one shoe.

"I don't want us to say goodbye", he said as he kissed her.

"Me neither, but we have to". She replied with tears in her eyes.

"Damn it...see I knew we shouldn't have...." she said

"Shush", replied Leo as he wiped her tears and kissed her again.

"Right, okay, this is what's gonna happen", said Leo.

"We ARE going to keep in touch, we ARE going to meet again....right?"

"Right", said Jasmine unconvincingly.

She picked up her bag and her other shoe. He held her hand tightly as he walked her to the door.

"Thank you for a wonderful, wonderful time Leo. Text me, Skype me, email me, the lot...please".

"I will", he replied with tears in his eyes as he pushed a strand of hair away from her face.

"Okay, I'm going to do the walk of shame back to the hotel...as I have been a bad girl", laughed Jasmine through tears rolling down her cheeks.

"You can watch me if you like", she said.

He kissed her again, she pulled away and walked out of the door.

"You are not bad, just very naughty", he said with a grin on his face.

As Jasmine started to walk away, Leo called after her.

"Jasmine, quick, come back".

"No... no... no, I have to go", she said as she turned to wave at him, whilst mopping her tears.

"Jasmine, stop", said Leo as he ran onto the beach, still in just a towel, to catch up with her.

He grabbed her arm and stopped her.

"Look, don't make this any harder Leo... I'll rip your towel off if you don't let go", she laughed.

He bent down and unpeeled a used condom that was stuck to the back of her leg.

"Shit", gasped Jasmine.

"I didn't want you to walk through the hotel lobby wearing this...although...it would have been extremely funny".

"Come here", he kissed her again on the cheek.

"Goodbye Leo"

"See ya soon Jas".

She turned and didn't look back. She was crying uncontrollably like a daft love struck teenager.

Chapter 22

The girls spent their last day of their holiday lazing and basking on the beach. The weather was a lot cooler and pockets of clouds had begun to gather in the November sky. There was a lot of activity around the resort as the locals were preparing for the annual Van's Triple Crown of Surfing competition that was coming up in the next few days. It was a Hawaiian specialty series of professional surfing events, offering three events to men and three events to women. For the men those events are the Reef Hawaiian Pro at Haleiwa Ali'i Beach Park; the O'Neill World Cup of Surfing at Sunset Beach; and the Billabong Pipeline Masters at the Banzai Pipeline. The women's events are the Vans Hawaiian Pro at Haleiwa Ali'i Beach Park; the Roxy Pro at Sunset Beach; and the Billabong Pro Maui at Honolua Bay, Maui. All events, with the exception of the women's Billabong Pro Maui, are staged on the North Shore of Oahu, world famous in surfing terms for its clockwork winter swells that reach fifty feet in height. The Vans Triple Crown of Surfing is second only to surfing's world title as it is considered to be the ultimate test of a surfer's ability to master the big waves at three unique venues, each with its own set of challenges for the surfer.

In addition to individual event champions, the Vans Triple Crown of Surfing crowns an overall men's and women's champion each year. This goes to the surfer who has performed best across all three competitions, making them the most proficient big-wave rider in the world.

The sea was buzzing with professional surfers practicing their manoeuvres and tricks and on the beach they were waxing and admiring their surfboards.

There was a slight chill in the breeze so the girls decided to pack up their belongings and head off to the Watershed Gift shop, which was on the resort, to get some last minute presents to take home.

"I have to get Alex a Ukulele", exclaimed Jasmine, "do you think he'll like it?"

"He will love it, but are you sure you can handle the racket he's going to make with it?" laughed Cerys.

The Watershed plays upon the concept of a North Shore water man's accessory shed, a place of pride in Hawaii's coastal communities where every water man and woman house their "tools" for maximizing their adventures. The Watershed features all locally designed and crafted custom fixtures – many cleverly created out of re-purposed local woods and materials.

The girls didn't know what to get, there was so much choice. After a lot of 'ooo-ing' and 'aaah-ing', they made their minds up with Cerys buying a silver bracelet with delicate hibiscus flower charms for Steph and an oversized surfing t-shirt for her dad. Jasmine decided she could put up with the racket and went ahead and bought Alex a ukulele and she bought her mum a painting of the sunset over the North shore, along with matching silver necklaces with a tasteful turtle charm for both her and Cerys.

"Here we are", said Jasmine handing Cerys a small gift box as they walked backed towards the hotel lobby carrying their beach bags and gifts.

"Wha's this for?" asked Cerys.

"Just a small gift for my bestest mate ever, and a reminder of our tremendous experience together. Look I've got one as well", said Jasmine as she dangled her necklace in front of Cerys' face.

"It's gorgeous mate", replied Cerys as she placed a sloppy kiss on Jasmine's cheek.

Back in their hotel suite the girls packed up some of their luggage before getting ready to go out for their last evening meal on the paradise island.

Jasmine was ready first, she wore a loose fitted three-quarter dress in pale pink with a thin white cardigan and a pair of white pumps that she hadn't had chance to wear. Her hair was scraped back off her face in a high ponytail. Cerys wore a pair of her white calf length jeans, which Jasmine thought looked a bit baggy on her, a turquoise vest top and matching cardigan. Jasmine couldn't take in how much weight Cerys seemed to have lost. Her hair hung down around her face and it seemed lank and thin and her eyes had dark shadows forming underneath. Jasmine hadn't noticed this before as Cerys wore her hair up mostly and seemed to wear sunglasses throughout most of the holiday. Both wore their new turtle charm necklaces.

"Are you okay Cerys?" asked Jasmine.

"Yes, now come on otherwise we will lose our table", she replied curtly.

"Al-right", tutted Jasmine as she picked up her bag, checking her phone to see if there was anything from Leo, knowing full well it would be a few more hours until he landed in Canada.

They arrived at the restaurant called 'Ola' which was situated on the beach, and means 'Life, living healthy and alive'. The tables were covered and surrounded with dramatic iron wood pillars and rafters which added to the natural beauty of the décor.

"Gawd Cerys, I don't know who many times I've said this but this is absolutely beautiful," exclaimed Jasmine as the girls were shown to their table which was facing the wild, rolling waves and pure soft, white sand.

They both ordered a Blue Hawaiian cocktail to start, which was filled with rum, pineapple juice, curacao, vodka, crème of coconut and an array of umbrellas and decorations.

Jasmine chattered on about Leo as Cerys quietly sipped her drink, occasionally rolling her eyes and smiling at the same time. She felt warm and happy that her friend had finally met someone, with a little help here and there from her.

They both read their menus and Cerys ordered the pan seared fresh island fish with summer vegetable ratatouille and Jasmine ordered the guava orange half chicken with ginger jasmine rice, just because her name was in it!

Jasmine wolfed her meal down as soon as it was set down in front of her, but Cerys picked at hers.

"What's wrong Cerys?" asked Jasmine as she took a breather from chewing. She placed her hand on top of Cerys'.

"Look, I know you're not right. You pick at your food, you look shattered all the time and you've lost weight whilst I've gained a little pot belly. You are swallowing tablets like they are going out of fashion whilst still drinking booze. Are you addicted to them? Is that what it is? If so I can help you mate".

Cerys withdrew her hand from under Jasmine's quickly.

"No, don't be daft, me an addict…tut…you silly mare. My tablets are very mild painkillers, it won't hurt having a drink with them. I'm hardly getting pissed every night am I? Look, I'm going through the menopause early, or something like that." She looked away at the ocean as she carried on.

"Pains in my back and stomach, that's what the tablets are for. I'm al-right honestly. I saw the doctor before we came here and he said I'm on the change, that's all. I'm a wuss when it comes to pain, that's why you can see it in my face and stuff."

"Hmm, well, as long as you're sure. You would tell me if there was something else wouldn't you?" quizzed Jasmine, not really sure if she believed her or not.

Cerys rolled her eyes, nodded and continued to pick at her meal.

After they had left the restaurant, they walked along the beach back towards the lobby. It started to drizzle lightly and with a mixture of sea spray the girls were getting wet so decided to go back to their suite with a bottle of champagne from the lobby bar to celebrate their last night.

Back at their suite, Jasmine changed in to her oversized bed t-shirt and Cerys into a pair of shorts and a vest. They snuggled up under a blanket on the lanai sipping champagne whilst watching the drizzle turn into a hard rain that bounced off the decking, Jasmine clutching her mobile phone, waiting for a message from Leo.

"Right, when we get back home, we'll start saving again to come back shall we? I can meet Leo here again and you can bring Steph, how about that?" asked

Jasmine, grinning as she placed her head on Cery's shoulder, pulling the blanket tightly round her with one hand and clasping her glass of champagne in the other.

Cerys smiled and kissed her friend on the top of her head. She didn't reply. They sat in silence, sipping their drinks and taking in the view.

"Well, I'm beat", yawned Cerys.

"C'mon missy, we have a long day ahead of us tomorrow," yawned Cerys.

She gave Jasmine a squeeze and went on to bed.

"Night-night", she shouted.

"Yep night -night, I'm going now in a minute", replied Jasmine.

She drained the bottom of her glass of champagne and headed off to bed as well. Just as she snuggled under the covers her phone beeped.

"Hey you gorgeous, beautiful and sexy creature, hope you have enjoyed your last day in paradise whilst I've been stuck in a flying tin can for the last ten hours. (Smiley face). Have landed safely, luggage collected and about to get into a cab. Sleep well and text me tomorrow. L xxxx"

"Who is this again? (Smiley face)", replied Jasmine.

"Forgotten me already hey. Well I had better turn my ass around and get back on the plane to remind you. (Smiley face). L xxx"

"Ha ha, glad you've arrived safely, I'm missing you sooo much. Want you now!!!!" replied Jasmine.

"Stop it, you are making me hard just thinking about you. Now go to sleep and I'll see you in your dreams. Oh, and no snoring right! L Xxx "

"Night night, will message you tomorrow. Mmmwoah. Jas. (Smiley face) xxx".

Jasmine drifted off to sleep gently with the biggest grin ever on her face, clutching her mobile phone tightly to her breast.

The girls said their goodbyes to the staff and other guests as they walked through the lobby dragging their luggage behind them the next morning. The trip to the airport was silent and the girls and the other passengers on the hotel transportation bus drank in the views of the heavenly island they were about to leave.
The flight to LA was smooth and seemed to go quickly. They had a quick change over to the flight to Cardiff. They didn't stay over this time. The night flight to Cardiff was bumpy and uncomfortable. They hit a few storms and experienced terrible turbulence.
Finally they arrived over British waters and waters was the correct term. It had rained so much over the last few days everything was water logged. The captain announced that there was a lot of water on the runway and that he would have to circle a few times whilst it was being cleared. Cerys drifted in and out of sleepiness, whilst Jasmine gripped tightly onto the arms of her seat.
"The devil is waiting for me", mumbled Cerys.
"What?" asked Jasmine.
"Ohh, sorry... dreaming", replied Cerys as she sat up promptly wiping the dribble from the corner of her mouth with the back of her hand.
Suddenly from the front of the plane a man started singing,
"The Green Green Grass of home", extremely loudly.

Everyone that knew it, including the girls and even the captain over his loud speaker, joined in.

The runway was clear and the plane began to land. As soon as it came to a standstill, everyone clapped.

After the girls had collected their luggage and had made it through customs, not that they had anything to hide, but there was always that worry for some unknown reason, they headed off to their cars.

Once their bags were loaded, they hugged each other ever so tightly, Cerys more so than Jasmine. It was as if she wasn't going to see her again. Jasmine felt a shiver down her spine.

"Right, shall we meet up for lunch next week sometime to reminisce?" asked Jasmine, rubbing Cerys' arm.

"Sounds good to me. I'll ring you soon. Love ya Jas. So long", said Cery's as she climbed into her car.

"Love ya back Cerys", waved Jasmine.

Chapter 23

Jasmine slept for what seemed like days when she arrived home, although it was only a few hours really. She was awoken by Ruby jumping on her bed and licking her face, wagging her tail furiously, and Bridget purring loudly and rubbing her head on her foot that was hanging out of the duvet cover.

"Hiya Jas, sorry love", shouted Olivia, Jasmine's mum, up the stairs.

"I tried to bring them in quietly but they couldn't wait to see you.

"Be down now mum", replied Jasmine, rubbing her eyes and cuddling both of her excited pets. Olivia had picked them both up from the kennels to save Jasmine having to do it, plus she missed them both as well. She treated them as if they were her grand-children.

"Look at the colour of you love. I must look as white and pale as a ghost", remarked Olivia as Jasmine walked down the stairs, quickly followed by Ruby and Bridget. She was wearing her pink, fluffy bathrobe.

She hugged her mum tightly.

"Aw mum, it was bloody lovely, all of it.....and I met a man", she winked.

Jasmine made them both a coffee and she told Olivia all about it. She showed her mum the photos of the beautiful scenery, the hotel and of course, Leo and his mates, and she gave her the painting she had bought for her.

"Aw love, I'm so pleased you had a good time Jas, you really deserve it lovely girl. This picture is stunning. Think I'll stick it in the kitchen...hmm", she pondered whilst admiring it.

"Now don't be doing anything daft like buggering off to Canada to chase 'im will you! Leave it as it is, a holiday romance, alright?"

"Yes mum", said Jasmine rolling her eyes at her.

"Right, better go, got yoga in half an hour and I want to get my spot at the front, cos if fat bloody Cath gets there first I won't be able to see anything with her big backside in the way. Glad you are home my beautiful girl, have missed you I have."

Olivia squeezed Jasmine's cheeks together and kissed her on her forehead.

"Ta-ra love, see you later. Now go back to bed you look knackered", shouted Olivia as she closed the front door behind her.

Jasmine rang Alex to say she was home, but it went to answer machine, so she left a message for him to ring her. He was probably at a gig or a party somewhere she thought.

She sent a text to Cerys,

"Hiya love, hope you are home okay. I have terrible jet lag, how about you? Give a kiss to Steph for me and see you soon, (smiley face), Jas xx"

Next she sent a text to Leo.

"Hey there gorgeous, how are you doing? I have terrible jet lag, flight was awful, glad to be back on terraferma. I could sleep for a million years. Just told my mum about you and she told me not to go chasing after you. Ha! Miss you lots. Text me when you can and we can arrange to Skype each other, okay. Jas xx"

Jasmine went back to bed feeling like all the blood had been drained out of her. Ruby and Bridget trotted along behind her and both cuddled up next to her, all snoring in harmony.

Several hours had passed and finally Jasmine awoke from her slumber. Ruby and Bridget were playing chase on the landing. She yawned and checked her phone.

There was a voice mail message from Alex, shouting as he was in a club saying he would be home the day after tomorrow with a pile of washing, and that he couldn't wait to see what present she had bought for him. Jasmine tutted and smiled as she listened to her son and heir really trying to say he had missed her.

There was no message from Cerys. Jasmine thought she was probably still sleeping or catching up with Steph in more ways than one.

Suddenly her phone beeped.

"Hey babes, glad you are home safely. It's freezing here, what's it like there? How about tomorrow to Skype? Can't wait to see you babe. Let me know what time is good for you. Off to see my agent in an hour, hopefully have an audition for a Christmas movie here in Ottawa. Fingers crossed. (Smiley face), Leo xxx".

"Hiya!! (smiley face with tongue out). Ooh good luck with the audition, looking forward to seeing you on the screen, (and in real life again)!!! I'm back in work tomorrow, sad face, so how about we Skype at 9pm my time? Is that okay? Jas xxx"

"Can't wait babe, see you tomorrow. L xxx"

Jasmine skipped around the house, closely followed by her excited pets, who thought it was a game, whilst grinning from ear to ear.

Nothing had changed back in work. The same old complaints of people abusing each other on social media sites. The, "he said, she said, I said, we said," and the, "what it is" conversations were all the same. She had opened up what seemed like a million emails to read. When it went quiet and none of the bosses were around, Jasmine slyly looked at her photos from her holiday. She sat with her elbows resting on the desk, chin in hand, (chins really as she had definitely put on a few pounds whilst she was away), sighing as she viewed the sexy pictures of Leo.

She jumped when the buzzer on the front counter was sounded.

"Hello, how can I help you", asked Jasmine as she hot footed it to the desk from the office.

Standing in front of her was a woman wearing a baseball cap and a long, black faux fur coat over a pair of blue pyjamas, waving her arms everywhere, whilst her daughter, who was dressed smartly in a grey trouser suit and white blouse sat calmly on the bench.

"Right I want something done, he went 'twitter' as she got out of 'er car. She didn't do anything love honest."

"What has happened?" asked Jasmine directing her question at the daughter.

"I told you love, he went 'twitter', replied the strangely dressed woman whilst pointing at her daughter.

Again, Jasmine looked directly at the daughter.

"Okay, you are going to have to give me a few more details. Firstly, what is your name?"

The mother went to reply but Jasmine held her hand up to shut her up.

The daughter stood up and walked towards Jasmine.

"My name is Jenna".

"Thanks Jenna, what has happened, and what does this lady mean when she said 'he went twitter'?"

Again the mother interrupted,

"You know, twitter", she said whilst demonstrating a punch.

"Aaaah, someone tried to hit you, is that right?"

Jenna nodded.

Finally, Jasmine managed to find out that Jenna had pulled out in front of someone in her car at the supermarket and cut them up causing the other driver to swerve. They both stopped and the other driver shouted at her. She went home and told her mother what had happened and her mother decided to frog march her to the station to report it and embellish the incident somewhat. She didn't want to make a complaint but the mother did, however, the mother wasn't even in the car at the time. The other driver never went 'twitter'. He just waved his arms in anger, words were exchanged, end of! The mother went on to ask what would have happened if this, or if that had happened, or if the other had happened. Jasmine wanted to say,

'If this, if that....if granny had balls she would be grandpa', but she didn't. They were both given suitable words of advice, Jenna mouthed the word 'Sorry' as she walked out behind her mother.

"Welcome back you jet setter", yelled Molly as she walked into the office to start her shift. She worked alongside Jasmine and was working the ten til eight shift.

She placed her handbag on her desk and gave Jasmine a big hug.

"C'mon then, tell me all about it".

Jasmine told her the ins and outs of her adventure and Molly sat there wide eyed, mouth open as she heard the story about Leo and Astrid.

She hadn't told her mother about Astrid as she knew it would have upset her.

"Bloody hell", replied Molly in her polite, posh, sweet Miss Money Penny voice. She sounded really funny when she swore, everyone said so.

Molly Knowles was about ten years older than Jasmine. She was married to Gerry who was a big, burly builder and they loved travelling. They had been all over the world and gave Jasmine loads of information about Hawaii before she went.

"So, let's see a picture of this chap then. You look positively glowing, I must say", said Molly.

Jasmine showed her the photos but they were soon interrupted by someone pressing the buzzer at the counter and the phones ringing off their hooks.

"Welcome back to reality", laughed Molly as she grabbed a pen, her spectacles and went to see the customers at the desk.

A little later on the other two Station Enquiry Officers popped in to see Jasmine. They were both on their rest days and out shopping in the town. They had bumped into each other and decided to pop into the station for a catch up and a cup of coffee as they didn't always all work together. Aiden Reubens was in his early fifties, married to Kay with two grown up children and three grandchildren and Lucy Burchell was in her late forties, married to Marc with one son and two step children. Each of them had their funny little sayings. Molly always replied,

"Happy to be here", when anyone ever asked her how she was. Lucy would say,

"You know what I mean", after statements she made, and Aiden would say,

"Ummm, well, I dunno", after he had mentioned a bit of gossip and wanted to dissociate himself from it straight away. Jasmine's little saying was,

"Keep buggering on", when things became challenging or difficult for her and her colleagues. She had 'borrowed' it from one of her favourite novels she had read several times and loved. They were a great little team and the neighbourhood officers nicknamed them 'Bosley and the Charlie Seven Angels', as the station radio call sign was 'Charlie Seven'.

Jasmine was exhausted from telling her holiday stories over and over again, but enjoyed reliving the bits about her meeting Leo though.

A queue started forming at the counter and the phones started ringing again.

"Right then, see you Thursday, the start of my shifts", sighed Aiden.

"Aye, and I'll see you on Saturday, when my shifts begin again", laughed Lucy.

Between them they called their working week 'shirts', relating to their uniform shirts, not shifts, because they didn't work the normal Monday to Friday or normal hours, as the station was open seven days a week and only closed on Bank Holidays, so they called their first shift, "shirt one". It seemed to make the week go quicker for some reason and it was a fantastic feeling when they made it to the last shirt. To see that last shirt taken off its hanger felt like they had conquered Mount Everest itself. They worked four, ten hour shifts and two nine hour shifts, six shirts in all, except for Molly who had taken flexible retirement and only worked five 'shirts'. It was a long week but wonderful when it came to their four rest days.

Chapter 24

Jasmine braced herself in front of the laptop, hair and make-up all done as if she was going on a date. The lamps were on and she lit a few candles to enhance the ambiance. Ruby was cuddled up to her on the sofa and Bridget sat behind her on the back of the sofa. She wore a sexy, off the shoulder thin sweater to show Leo what he was missing. She didn't bother with the bottom bit as he wouldn't see her from the waist down so she wore her fleecy and comfy pyjama bottoms. She had a glass of wine on standby to calm the nerves. She felt excited, but very nervous waiting for Leo to call her on Skype. The lap top rang and displayed incoming call from Leo. They both spoke at the same time, then paused, again spoke at the same time then laughed nervously in sync.

"Hey, I'll go first..... oh my Gawd you look more gorgeous than I remember", said Jasmine.

"Well hey sexy, you look amazing. How was work?" replied Leo.

"It was like I had never been away. Great to catch up with my colleagues though. How about the audition, how did it go"?

"Okay I think, I should know within a few days if they want me. Hey, I'm missing you, I can't stop thinking about you, is that mad? We haven't really known each other that long have we? I feel like I've known you for ages. I can't get that image of you walking on the beach with a Johnny stuck to your leg, and you falling backwards off your chair when we first met...so funny. I keep laughing out loud in random places thinking about it. People were looking at me strange when I did it in the queue of my local coffee shop earlier."

"It wasn't funny, well maybe for you, but not for me. Maybe you feel like you've known me longer because you and Cerys were scheming behind my back for months", laughed Jasmine.

"How is Cerys..... the pimp? She told me you called her that", grinned Leo.

"Well, I'm not sure. She didn't seem too well when we said our goodbyes at the airport. Mind you, she didn't seem that well the last couple of days of the holiday and to be honest, I'm not going to lie to you, I'm starting to get a bit worried. I have rang her and text her but no answer and no reply, I dunno. I'll try her again tomorrow. I know she has a few more leave days than me so maybe she and Steph made plans."

"What do you mean, to be honest, I'm not going to lie to you"? laughed Leo.

"Just a daft expression, nothing meant, us Welsh people love to fill a sentence with more words than necessary.... to be fair", smirked Jasmine.

"I'll remember that! Well, hope she is okay, and tell her I said 'Hi'. I will send her a message tomorrow as well".

They chatted for hours and hours. Leo placed his hand on the screen of his computer and Jasmine did the same on hers, placing her hand over the top of his, palm to palm. They stared at each other in silence. No words were necessary. They both felt the same. Her heart raced, she wanted him so badly it hurt.

They arranged to chat again in the next few days. As they were saying goodbye, Leo blushed and mouthed the words, "I love you" and then he was gone.

Jasmine sat staring at the blank screen.

"I love you too.....I think...it may be lust but I still want you", she said out loud as she closed her laptop screen, hoping he had disconnected and not heard a word of that. She couldn't remember what it felt like to be in love. She drained the bottom of her wine glass and went to bed.

All through the next day, whilst in work, Jasmine tried to ring and text Cerys, still no answer. She left messages upon messages to call her back. She also rang and left messages on Steph's phone.

After her shift she decided to drive to Cerys' house in Swansea. Alex was at home now, eating everything in sight, using all the electricity and hot water, so he was there to sort the pets out. It was a good hour's drive and the rain and wind still hadn't relented. She finally arrived, after many diversions because of fallen trees, to find the house all in darkness. Cerys' car was on the drive but Steph's wasn't. She knocked and rang the bell, looked through the window and even climbed over the fence to have a look around the back. No-one was in. She wrote a note and posted it through the letter box before heading back home. She wrote;

"Cerys, Steph, where the bloody hell are you? Hope you are both okay. I am really worried, I mean reeeeally worried. Please ring me or text me as soon as you can. Lots of love, Jas xxx".

Jasmine finally arrived home. She stopped off on the way to buy fish and chips for her and Alex.

The sound of loud guitar riffs echoed from upstairs, the cat and dog were stretched out over the sofa, the radiators were on full blast, it was like a sauna in the room, shoes were strewn over the kitchen floor.

"Alex, I'm home", yelled Jasmine as she turned the heating right down and kicked the shoes towards the patio doors, out of the way.

No reply, Alex was playing his guitar at full pelt and the amp was on maximum.

"Aleeeex", she yelled again.

Still no answer.

Jasmine turned the electric off at the trip switch.

"SHIT", yelled Alex

"Alex, I'm home, thank goodness that row has stopped. Come and have some food", shouted Jasmine at the top of her lungs whilst turning the electricity back on.

"You scared the life out of me mam", said Alex as he ran into the kitchen where Jasmine was serving up their fish and chips.

"Good, that'll teach you not to play so bloody loud won't it", she replied.

"How is aunty Cerys then? Thought you would be home a lot later than this"

"I gathered that by the bloody racket you were making. Lucky Mrs Daniels next door is as deaf as a post and the other side is empty otherwise someone would have called the police. She wasn't in. Very strange. Hope she is alright".

"It wasn't that loud mun", said Alex whilst shovelling handfuls of chips in his gob, completely disregarding the answer to his question about Cerys.

The house phone rang urgently at 3am. Jasmine jumped out of her skin. She grabbed the phone quickly from the bedside cabinet before it woke Alex up.

"Hello"

"Hi Jas, its Steph," it went silent.

"Steph, what's happened, are you okay?" Jasmine sat up in bed with a start.

"Yes, well no. Its Cerys, she is really unwell. She is in hospital. Has been for a couple of days. Sorry, I only just picked up your note and messages now, not had time to do anything. Sorry". Steph started to cry.

"Steph, oh my Gawd, what's the matter with Cerys"?

"When she came home from the airport she went straight bed. I thought it was just jet lag. I unpacked her suitcase and bags and found a couple of bottles of prescription pills, some full, some empty. When she woke up I asked her about it. She looked awful Jas, she had a job to put one foot in front of the other. She appeared to be in so much pain. She told me the tablets were for the menopause, she said she had started it early or something and it was causing her problems. She collapsed in the bathroom, so I called an ambulance. She has been in hospital for the last few days. She has ovarian cancer Jas. She has known about it for ages and didn't tell anyone as far as I know, well not me or her dad anyway. She lied to us. The tablets were to control the pain".

Steph started to cry uncontrollably.

Jasmine took a large gulp. She couldn't believe it. Her whole body began to shake and tears slowly began to drop down her cheeks.

"Steph, oh Gawd, why didn't she bloody say anything. I can't believe it."

Jasmine wiped her tears and coughed.

"We will get her through this, loads of people survive this don't they?" said Jasmine positively.

"It had already spread through her liver and lungs when she was first diagnosed. She wasn't well for a while, but you know Cerys, she can't be arsed with the doctors and will just battle through any illness or injury. Remember when she broke her wrist in work? She wouldn't go to the hospital until her Sergeant dragged her there. Just before she went to Hawaii, she went to the hospital after finally seeing the doctor and they diagnosed her then. She was advised not to travel but told them bluntly where to go, you know what she is like. She told them she was going if it was the last thing she did! Seems like it was..... I didn't know, I swear. I would have stopped her going and looked after her. Stubborn cow. She knew it was too late to be treated. She was offered all the treatment but was told it was terminal and the treatment would only give her a few months anyway, so she declined it and wanted to make the most of the time she had left. She wanted to go on holiday with you more than anything, with all the secret calls and plotting, she was determined. She told me all this after the doctor had seen her, when she was admitted to hospital. I'm still in shock Jas."

Jasmine was choking back the tears. She couldn't believe it. Her best friend was going to die and she didn't tell her. She really couldn't believe this was happening.

"How long... how long has she....when?" she couldn't say the words.

"Weeks, maybe less. Oh Jas, I don't know what to do, I feel helpless. Her dad is with her now. We have been taking it in turns to sit with her. She is coming home tomorrow as she wants to be in comfortable surroundings. They will bring her in an ambulance and a nurse will be appointed to take care of her. She asked me to tell you and said to say sorry.

"Steph, I'm coming over now. Let me get dressed, I'll be there as soon as I can."

"No Jas, no. It's late, it's too far. I'm okay. I need to try and sleep to get some energy to look after my beautiful girl tomorrow", she sobbed.

"I'll come straight from work tomorrow then, is that okay".

"Yes, that's fine. Sorry to drop this on you."

"I....I just can't believe it Steph".

Jas couldn't sleep. She sobbed and cried all night. She felt numb.

Chapter 25

Steph and Cery's dad went to the kitchen to make coffee, leaving Jasmine and Cerys talking in the bedroom.

Cerys looked gaunt, tired, worn out. She was weak. Her lips were dry and it was an effort for her to speak.

Jasmine stroked Cerys' forehead and hugged her friend closely. She couldn't believe that less than a week ago they were having fun in paradise.

Cerys must have been really struggling whilst they were away, putting on a brave face, trying to keep it together. She disguised it so well, Jasmine thought to herself.

"Why didn't you tell me love? You must have been in so much pain?" asked Jasmine, feeling the sting of carefully suppressed tears.

"Cos, I knew what you would be like. I did it for me as well as you. Leo begged me to tell you but I couldn't".

"Wait a minute, Leo knew?" said Jasmine as she sprang upright from cuddling her friend.

"I wasn't sure if he would meet us if I didn't tell him, so I used it...sorry love, but it worked out perfectly, so don't stress about it," replied Cerys with a strained smile as she reached out to pick up a glass of water from the bedside cabinet.

"So, the only reason he met us was because he felt sorry for you. So it was all fake, you lied to me, he lied to me. I'm losing my closet friend in the whole wide world. I let my guard down, gave my heart to a guy I didn't really know, only to find out that he did it out of pity. That's it, he can bugger off. I want someone who wants me for me being me, not cos my friend is dying. I just can't believe this," said Jasmine crossly. "Shit I sound like a right selfish mare...sorry mate."

"Shut up, he really likes you, he didn't just meet you cos I'm dying he did it cos he wanted too. I threw it in the mix, just in case, a sob story always works but I didn't need it", replied Cerys, using all her strength to speak.

"How do you know?"

"I just do alright".

Cerys held Jasmine's hand and gently drifted off to sleep. Jasmine kissed the back of Cerys' hand and placed it gently under the warm duvet.

She said her goodbyes to Cery's dad and Steph and said she would be back again tomorrow.

She paced around the kitchen when she arrived home. She didn't know how to cope. She couldn't relax.

Her phone beeped. Text from Leo.

"Hey there, my little Welsh cake. See, I have been busy researching a land I know not much of!!! Hope all is good over there. Any news from Cerys??? Let me know when we can speak next over the laptops. I have loads to tell you. Can't wait. All the best, Leo. (Smiley face),xxxx."

Jasmine felt too angry to reply. Her emotions were all mixed up.

"Any news from Cery's?" Jasmine read out loudly. "Of course there is, you KNOW what the news is, you scheming, lying......oooooh." She couldn't finish her sentence, she didn't reply, she was too annoyed.

Jasmine woke up the next morning, before work, to a string of text messages from Leo.

"I'm so sorry, Cerys has contacted me and told me that you know. I couldn't tell you, I wanted too but I couldn't. I was sworn to secrecy. You must be feeling awful. Sorry babe. I really... I mean REALLY, like you. I would have met up with you anyway, not just cos of Cerys. I liked the messages you sent to me on Face book, I enjoyed reading them and felt like I wanted to get to know you way before Cerys and I ever spoke. I didn't realise how sick she was. Please let me know you are alright, PLEASE!!!

Leo xxxxxx".

She was still too angry and still in shock. She didn't know what to believe. She couldn't reply.

Jasmine visited Cerys after work for the next few evenings and spent her rest days with her, reading to her, snuggled up watching old films. She had ignored all of Leo's messages and calls. He was the last thing on her mind, Cerys was more important. He wouldn't give up. It gave Steph and Cerys' dad a rest with her being there as well. After watching, "Monty Python's, The Life of Brian", Jasmine dozed off next to Cerys who had fallen asleep not long after the opening credits. They lay side by side holding hands.

Jasmine was awoken gently by Steph tapping her shoulder. Her face was awash with tears.

"She's gone, Jas", she whispered, choking on her tears.

Jasmine turned towards Cerys.

"No... Cerys".

Her hand she was holding was cold. She looked peaceful and the pain had gone from her face.

Jasmine and Steph, in turn, kissed Cerys' forehead and left the room so her dad could be with her. The grief they both felt was unimaginable.

The days leading up to Cerys' funeral were a blur for Jasmine. She wasn't living, she was just existing. She still hadn't contacted Leo, even though he kept leaving her messages every day. The end of November was looming. It was dark and miserably cold. She felt lost and lonely again, a feeling she was familiar with after experiencing it once before when her marriage broke down. She couldn't stand being without her mate, her best friend. Her work colleagues and her Sergeant were a great support. They had all worked with Cerys so they felt Jasmine's sadness as well.

Jasmine sat in the second row with her mum and Alex at the crematorium, behind Cerys and Steph's family. It was packed out with police officers and police staff, work colleagues, and friends. Just before they had gathered inside, six police officers from Cery's shift, two women and four men, carried her coffin in on their shoulders. All of them struggled to hold back their sadness. Soft music played in the background. The music was, "You Raise Me Up", by Josh Groban. Cerys' dad had chosen it. It was the only input he was allowed to have. The officers carrying the coffin were dressed in their 'number one' uniforms. They looked extremely smart wearing their white shirts, black ties, tunics, razor pressed trousers and shiny boots, normally kept for special occasions and court. The coffin was draped with the flag and emblem of the Welsh Police Force and Cerys' police hat was proudly placed on top with a bouquet of yellow roses, her favourite flower.

The police officers walked slowly in time with the music and gently placed the coffin at the altar. There was a quiet murmur of people talking as they gathered in their seats. Some had to stand at the back as the seats had all been taken.

All went silent as the minister began to speak.

"I am the resurrection and the life, said the Lord. Those who believe in me, even though they will die, will live, and everyone who lives and believes in me, will never die. John 11.25.26.

We meet in the name of Jesus Christ, who died and was raised to the glory of God the Father. Grace and Mercy be with you.

We have come here today to remember before God our sister, Cerys Roden, to give thanks for her life, to commend her to God our merciful redeemer and judge, to commit her body to be cremated and to comfort one another in our grief".

Cerys' dad and Steph both gripped each other tightly. The grief overtook them and they began to sob uncontrollably. Alex and Olivia both held Jasmine's hands to comfort her as her whole body began to shake.

The minister carried on.
"Let us pray.

Almighty God, you judge us with infinite mercy and justice, and love everything you have made. In your mercy turn the darkness of death into the dawn of new life, and the sorrow of parting into the joy of Heaven; through our saviour, Jesus Christ, Amen."

The Hymn that was chosen by Cerys was 'Amazing Grace'. Everyone sang it out loud and proud for her.

The minister then called upon Cerys' dad to do a reading. He read, "The Lord is my shepherd", but broke down half way through and Steph courageously took over. Cerys didn't want the story of her life to be read out. She thought that everyone she knew and loved knew all that anyway. Cerys' Sergeant stood up next. He stood tall and straight, his well-earned metal stripes glistened in the light that streamed through the window.

"Hello everyone, I'm Sergeant Robbins. I have been Cerys' supervisor for the last six years. She was a wonderful, hardworking, conscientious, highly regarded officer who was also strong, funny, mischievous a great friend and colleague.

She hid my hat one day just as we were about have a visit from you Sir", he pointed at the Chief Constable who was sat a few rows back. "The Chief wanted to spend a night shift with us, walking the beat, but Cerys thought it would be extremely funny to hide my tall hat. I had to borrow PC Cob's hat. It was the only one that wasn't locked away or being used. Those of you who know PC Cob know that he has a massive head. I looked like I had a bucket on my head. I told the Chief, when he questioned me about it being so big, that I had lost a lot of weight recently. I didn't want to drop PC Roden in it… Sorry Sir", he gestured to the Chief

Constable again. "I know you didn't believe me. I made Cerys do foot patrol for a month as punishment after that, but she didn't mind. She didn't sulk like a lot of them would have done. She loved it. She gathered fantastic intelligence from being out there talking to people instead of driving around in the panda. I never found my hat. We will miss you PC 900 Roden. God Bless you."

There was a quiet laugh amongst the congregation.

Sergeant Robbins saluted the coffin and then saluted Cerys' family before sitting back in his seat.

The Chief Constable then stood up.

"We are here to remember PC 900 Cerys Roden, an outstanding officer of great honesty, integrity and bravery. She was a wonderful officer, a great listener, fun loving so I have heard, but always very professional and I am extremely proud to have served with her. She was all about people and the community and I know she will be a huge loss, not just to her family, but to the community she served. As you know the entrance to the Police station has been covered in flowers from people in the community who knew her.

I first met her when I was on the board for Sergeants promotions, many years ago. Those of you who know her, remember she passed her part one of her Sergeants exam but never went on to do the board and I believe I know the reason why. Many years ago, I was on the panel for the mock boards. The mock boards were a run through or a practice session prior to the actual boards in those days, we no longer do that now. Anyway, Cerys came in for her mock Sergeants board. Although it wasn't the real thing, it was still tense. She sat down, legs crossed, quite nervous to start but slightly more relaxed once the questions and answers began to flow. After about two hours the session was complete. She was thanked and was advised she could leave. She stood up but collapsed straight on the floor. Her leg had gone numb from being crossed so long. None of us on the panel said anything. We wanted to laugh but knew that we couldn't. She gathered herself together, brushed herself down, thanked anyone and promptly walked to the door, opened it and then shut it behind her, Again, the panel and I just sat there in silence, crying with laughter inside. A few moments later she emerged from behind that door and went to the correct door and left. She had gone in to the large store cupboard, stayed there for a few minutes, waited as if none of us had noticed. I have to say, it made us laugh all day long after that. I can see why she didn't come back to sit the real board. She would have made a wonderful Sergeant if she had. Her mock board exam was excellent, until the end that is."

Everyone smiled and again quietly and respectfully laughed.

The Chief carried on.

"Cerys asked me to read a poem that she had adapted, when I visited her at home. She was given the inspiration by another police officer from Greater Manchester Police, in honour of two fallen colleagues in the line of duty. She had read it a while ago and it really moved her. It summed up the day in the life of a bobby and she wanted others to be remembered as well as her.

The alarm clock rings loudly, it's early dawn.
I stretch out my arms and let out a yawn.

As I tie up my boots I think ahead,
In about fifteen hours time I can go back to my bed.
Quietly I close and lock the front door,
And climb into my car, I don't have to be quiet anymore.
Radio on full blast as I drive down the road,
What will the day bring, I wonder as I shudder from the early morn cold.
I pull up outside the station I love,
So proud to work there, I can't say enough,
Vest and appointments on and to the briefing room I go,
To my colleagues and friends, banter in full flow.
To serve and protect in every single way,
Briefing over, off we go to face the challenges of the day.
Patrolling around, enquiries to be made,
Waiting for the calls, and we are on our way.
"Emergency incident", the operator calls,
I respond "en route" without a murmur or a pause.
In a flash I arrive in front of the house,
A colleague arrives, "wait for me", she shouts.
Calmly we enter and call out "hello",
A large figure appears, "Oh God, no".
The bang was so loud, I drop to the floor,
Eyes searching for my colleague,
Then I can see no more.
Cold and dark, I fade away,
Why did this become that dreaded day.
My family, my life, it's all gone,
But I'm very proud of all the things that I have done.
I've seen and done things that most people fear,
For my job and my badge that I hold so dear.
I'm a partner, a friend, a daughter too,

Not just a uniform, a person like you.

Regrets I have none, service to the public I willingly gave,
Day in day out, I never thought I was brave.
Now I patrol and walk the Pearly Gates beat,
Watching over all and new friends I must meet.
Please remember me, in briefing I once sat,
The girl who happened to wear a bobby's hat.
(Poem inspired by PC Amie Holland, Bolton Division, Greater Manchester Police)

"PC Roden asked me to say to all her family, colleagues and friends, be safe, be kind, look after each other, thank you for looking after her family in this time of sadness, please continue to support them ...or else. She loves you, well some of you, will miss you, again some of you all.....I didn't write this honestly.... and she goes on to say...see you on the other side. She will be waiting for us all with a pint in her hand, but she doesn't want to see any of us for a long long time. Live long and prosper....oh dear...may the force be with you. God Bless you all…well some of you."

Everyone laughed again.

The Chief saluted Cerys' coffin and her family, shook her dad's hand, kissed Steph's cheek and sat back down.

The minister finished the ceremony with the Lord's Prayer. As the coffin went off behind the curtain and the mourners were lead out, the music started to play. It was Monty Python's "Always look on the bright side of life", from "The Life of Brian". The last film Cerys and Jasmine watched together. It was as if she knew.

Everyone made their way to the wake, or the 'bun fight' as Cerys called it. The Police officers who were on duty and the Chief, said their goodbyes to the family and left to carry on with the job that Cerys so dearly loved. The average sized room above at The Greyhound pub was full of friends, family and well-wishers. A buffet was laid out ready and the staff offered everyone a free glass of wine as they walked in. Olivia and Alex linked their arms with Jasmine's as she felt very unsteady as they walked up the steep stairs to the room. She felt as if her head was all muzzy, as if she was walking on cotton wool. Her sorrow had almost consumed her. Her heart felt heavy and her mood, sombre. They sat down at a table in the corner of the room and Alex brought their drinks over.

"To Cerys," said Olivia has she held her glass up, whilst looking up at the heavens, or the ceiling in this case.

"Don't be daft, she won't be up there", said Steph as she walked by, with mascara smudged eyes, and a strained smile.

"You know she was a bit of a girl and a half". She patted Olivia on the shoulder and headed off towards Cery's dad.

"To Cerys", repeated Alex and Jasmine. Alex placed his hand on top of his mum's to comfort her.

Cery's dad tapped the microphone that was on a small stage at the back of the room. Steph was beside, him holding his hand tightly.

"Umm, hello, hello everyone. Thank you very much for coming. Help yourself to the buffet. I'm sorry there is only one free glass of wine each, my beautiful daughter didn't want to indulge you too much, she said she had better things for her well earned money to go too and besides, the staff here have offered to donate ten percent of the bar takings to cancer research, so drink up. Anyway, please everyone, raise a glass to my daughter. Please celebrate her life."

He paused, gulped and started to shake, then continued whilst hugging Steph closely.

"Sorry, like I said, celebrate her love for life, and live each day like it's your last......Cerys". He raised his glass high and everyone did the same.

"Nos da cariad, goodnight love".

Light, soft music started playing in the background and the mourners began to mingle and gather around the buffet. The murmurs became louder the more they had to drink. Jasmine couldn't drink, she sipped her glass of wine slowly, staring blankly around the room. Alex and Olivia went to the buffet, Alex stuffed the food in his mouth at the same time as loading his plate under the disgraced look and watchful eye of his grandmother, who slapped his wrist when he tried to answer her back with a mouthful of scotch egg.

Jasmine wandered over to Steph and Cery's dad.

"Oh my Gawd, I don't know Cerys' dad's name", she suddenly stopped in her tracks. After all these years of knowing Cerys she had never heard his name…how odd. Cerys had introduced him as, "this is my dad", Steph always called him 'dad'. She felt flushed and embarrassed.

"Well come on, introduce us", said a voice from behind her. Olivia and Alex were stood close by. Alex had a mountain of food on his plate and Olivia was delicately nibbling on a vol-au-vent.

Before Jasmine could open her mouth Cerys' dad stepped forward.

"I'm Steve, and this is Steph".

There it was, Steve...'Phew' thought Jasmine.

"I'm Olivia and this is my grandson and Jasmine's son Alex".

Alex wiped his hand on his trousers and held out his hand to offer a shake. Steve greeted Jas and Olivia with a hug. They spoke for a long while about the service, the speeches and how proud they all were. Steve pointed out the buffet to people as they approached him with their kind words and attempted to guide Steph, Olivia and Jasmine there too. He slowly edged his way to the table hoping they would all follow. Jas and Steph stayed where they were. They didn't feel like eating anything.

Olivia and Steve walked off chatting away. Alex devoured everything on his plate from a second helping, kissed his mother on her cheek and asked if it was alright to go. He felt a bit awkward and he had scoured the room for talent or anyone remotely his age but failed. She said yes and gave him some money for a taxi. Steph hugged Jasmine so tightly she felt as if her buttons on her dress would pop.

"What are we going to do without her Jas?" she said, gently touching her forehead with hers and holding her hands.

"We have to go on Steph. She wouldn't want us to mope around. I bet she is watching us right now, tutting and f-ing and blinding at us."

"You're right", laughed Steph, "but it's going to be hard".

"I know love, I know". Jasmine hugged her again.

Olivia and Steve chatted for what seemed like ages. Olivia told him she was divorced from Jasmine's dad Eric, who was a plumber but now retired. Their love just fizzled out, they had no shared interests and hardly spent any time together. She told him he went to live in Weymouth after their divorce and Jasmine hardly saw him as he had bought a little boat and was off sailing here and there most of the time. Olivia lived alone after her divorce. Her son Peter, Jasmine's brother, was an I.T executive and lived in China with his wife Elaine. She hadn't seen him in ages as he hadn't been home for a while. She decided to get a dog for company called Flo, an Italian Spinone gun dog, who never left her side. She worked in an office at a publishers for years but her greatest love was art. She loved to paint and draw and became quiet established after selling a few to a local gallery and on the internet, so she decided to take her redundancy from her office job and paint and create pottery full time. She had her own little studio in her garden and made quite a good living out of it. She was now semi-retired. She did the odd painting here and there to sell but did it mostly for her own enjoyment and she could please herself with her time, which she loved.

Steve told Olivia he was a green grocer. He had his own shop in the little village where he lives. It was his father's shop and his father's before him. His dad was known as Vic the veg two, and his grandfather was Vic the veg one. Steve's middle name was also Victor and he is still known locally as Vic the veg three. He wanted to call Cerys Victoria when she was born to carry on the name but her mother refused. Steve said Cerys never wanted to take over the shop she always wanted to be a police officer, ever since he could remember. It was lucky really as he would have been bankrupt if she carried on into the family business. When she used to help him out after school and during the holidays, she used to munch her way through most of the fruit and some of the veg.

"She was a bugger for peas in the pod, and celery", he remembered fondly.

Steve told Olivia that Cerys' mum was knocked over on a zebra crossing by a man who had a heart attack at the wheel of his car. He lost control and ploughed straight into her. She died there and then. Poor Cerys was only five at the time and he had to bring her up on his own.

"Tragic......now this". Steve wiped the tears away as Olivia cuddled him.

"Hi Jas, how you doing babes?" said a voice from an approaching group of friends. It was Molly from work. She was with Lucy and Aiden and also Ginger the cleaning lady and Mickey the driver-handyman from the station. Ginger was named after Ginger Rogers. Her father had been madly in love with the famous actress and dancer of the Hollywood glamour era.

"What a beautiful service, and wasn't that really nice of the Chief to do a speech, you know what I mean", remarked Lucy.

"It was, I have to say", replied Aiden. "C'mon, Jas let's get you a proper drink is it? Bloody wine is no good for you. You look like you could do with something to put some colour back in your cheeks girlie."

Aiden bought a round of whiskey shots for the friends. All of them slugged it back quickly and all of them coughed and spluttered as they did.

"I need the loo", coughed Jasmine as she rushed off quickly.

She threw up instantly. She hadn't eaten properly for days and her stomach couldn't take a whiskey on an empty tank. She wiped her mouth with a tissue, put the lid down on the loo, sat down and held her head in her hands.

"Oh Cerys, I miss you.", again the tears began to flow. "I hope you are okay, where ever you are. I wish you could give me a sign that it's going to be alright", she whispered under her breath.

"Ouch", she yelled out as the toilet roll holder cover dropped down from its hinges on the wall on to her head. She pushed it up and locked it.

"Ouch", she yelled for the second time as it fell again.

"How the hell is it dropping down?" she pushed it up again examining it as she did.

"OOOUch, you have got to be kidding me", for the third time it dropped and banged her on the head.

She sat smirking to herself with her right hand holding the cover so it didn't drop again and her left hand rubbing the bump it had created.

"Cerys..... thanks for that sign you bitch. Couldn't you have left a white feather or something like other angels do...oh that's right, you're not an angel, well not yet anyway." She blew a kiss into the air, went out of the cubicle, stared at herself in the mirror, washed her face and wiped her eyes and went back to join everyone else. She began to feel a sense of relief and calmness. She knew that must have been Cerys in there banging her head, it was the type of thing she would do, but most of all she felt as if she was happy and free from pain. It was a comfort for Jasmine.

She stood by the door and looked around the room. How blessed was Cerys to have known so many people. More to the point, how blessed were they to have known Cerys. She smiled to herself and headed towards Steph who was talking to a very attractive lady with beautiful strawberry blonde wavy hair. She had the curves of Jessica Rabbit.

"Jas, this is Maria", said Steph. "She used to be a police officer years ago, don't know if you knew her. Anyway, decided it wasn't for her and went back to train as a primary school teacher. I have to thank her really as you see, Maria and Cerys were an item once but decided to split up when Maria moved away to go back to university. Then a few months later Cerys and I got together".

"Oh, right, yes I remember Cerys telling me about you. Lovely to meet you Maria. I didn't get to work with you as you were at a different station weren't you?" replied Jasmine whilst rubbing her sore forehead.

"Yes I worked at HQ on traffic for a bit so never made it up to the Valleys much. Are you alright, your forehead is a bit red?"

"Yes, I'm fine, just had a bit of a row with the toilet roll holder cover", she smiled.

The music began to play a little louder and the bar manager asked everyone to take to the dance floor in honour of Cerys.

"Oh Gawd, I bet she has picked something by the Sex Pistols", Jasmine whispered to Steph.

"Ha-ha, no...she wanted to make sure she was remembered in song as well, always the centre of attention, my beautiful girl was."

'Unforgettable' by Nat King Cole started off the dancing. Steve took hold of Olivia's hand had gently put his hand around her waist. They swayed slowly in rhythm together. Maria and Steph took to the floor as well. Aiden, Lucy, Molly and Ginger formed a circle, holding each other's waists, grabbing Jas as they tastefully swayed to the music, thinking of Cerys.

"Someone to watch over me", by Linda Ronstadt was the next piece of music to follow. Everyone sang and swayed together in a large circle as if they were at a concert and Cerys was the star act. Jasmine clutched Steve and Steph tightly around the waist as they sang.

Eventually, people began to gather their coats and jackets, laughing and joking shouting the old Welsh saying, "Whose coat is this jacket". Steve and Steph thanked them for coming.

"Are you ready love?" asked Olivia as she wrapped her warm thick winter coat around her shoulders. "I've ordered a taxi so it won't be long".

"Yep, let's get a bit of air whilst were are waiting shall we", replied Jasmine.

They said their farewells to Cerys' family, but as they were about to go through the door, Steve shouted,

"Wait", Steph followed him closely as he hot footed it towards them.

"I almost forgot until Steph reminded me. Cerys asked me to give you this. We know what's in it but don't open it yet. You know she loved you like a sister don't you?"

He handed her a brown A4 sized envelope with Jasmine written on the front.

"Yes...and I her, but..." replied a shocked Jasmine.

"Don't ask us, just read it...it will make us all very happy. Now see you soon love".

"Thank you...yes see you soon. I'll phone you tomorrow alright?".

Olivia and Jasmine huddled together by the door of the pub waiting for their taxi to arrive. It was refreshing outside in the evening air. The rain had stopped but the breeze was icy.

"I wonder what this is?" said Jasmine to her mum.

"Put it in your bag safely and have a look when you get home", ordered Olivia.

"Do you know what it is?" she asked.

Before she could answer a taxi pulled up to the kerb.

"At last", shivered Olivia, but as they stepped forward, a man opened the door, stepped out with a small holdall bag, paid the driver and the taxi drove off.

"Oh bum, thought that was ours then. Never mind, let's get back under the shelter", remarked Olivia as she stepped backwards.

"Jasmine?" asked the man who had stepped out of the taxi.

"Yes", she answered. She stepped forward under the street light to see who it was.

"Leo....what are you doing here?"

Chapter 26

Dressed in a black suit, white shirt and a black tie he walked towards Jasmine. He donned a five o'clock shadow and his hair was slightly longer, which made him look even more handsome than she remembered.

"I tried to get to the funeral but my flight was delayed so I came straight here. Just in time by the looks of it".

"How did you know about the funeral and why have you come all this way?" asked Jasmine. Her stomach was jumping with butterflies. She felt excited, dizzy and anxious all at the same time.

"Steph, contacted me on Cerys' request. She invited me to come and I wanted too. I wanted to pay my respects......and I wanted to see you, so so much. I needed to straighten things out and because you wouldn't return my calls or answer my messages, this was the only way. I'm sorry I missed the service".

He placed his holdall on the ground and took Jasmine in his arms.

"I haven't stopped thinking about you since we met".

Too late, she surrendered. Everything she thought about him pitying her, arranging to meet just because Cerys told him she was ill, all disappeared into the crisp and frosty night air. She kissed him, he kissed her back. The tears trickled down her cheeks as she gazed into his eyes, and he gently wiped them away.

"Huhhmmm", coughed Olivia in the background.

"Oooh...Mum, this is Leo, Leo this is Olivia, my mum".

"Pleased to meet you Leo, you must be shattered after such a long flight. Where are you staying?" said Olivia as they shook hands.

"Pleased to meet you ma'am. Well, Steph said I could stay with her if I wanted too". He looked at Jasmine, hoping she would say something.

"No don't be daft, you are coming home with me", smiled Jasmine.

The taxi finally arrived. Olivia sat in the front with the driver and Leo and Jasmine sat closely together in the back. Jasmine couldn't help feeling daft and stupid after the appalling way she had treated Leo. She couldn't believe he had travelled all this way. Nothing further was said about it that night. Leo knew why she hadn't contacted him, but he wasn't annoyed. He understood. Cerys had contacted him when she had left hospital. Just a very quick phone call, aided by Steph.

Jasmine sent a text message to Steph explaining that Leo was with her and she ended it with a huge thank you and lots of daft smiley faces. Steph replied that she was pleased and would speak with her the following day. Olivia was dropped off at her home by the taxi first, then the 'couple' were dropped off a Jasmine's house a few minutes later. Alex had gone on to bed. His suit jacket was left hanging on the back of a chair in the kitchen and his size twelve shoes were left at the bottom of the stairs. Bridget was proudly squashed into one of them, snoozing away. Ruby was asleep was on the sofa. She wagged her tail just enough to say hello but was far too tired to move from her comfortable position.

"Do you want a drink or anything?" asked Jasmine as she took off her coat and hung her handbag on the bannister at the bottom of the stairs.

Leo didn't reply. He placed his hands tightly around her waist and drew her closely to his body. She began to breathe heavily. He kissed her tenderly to start with. The natural, manly scent of his body mixed in with the remnants of aftershave was overpowering. He gently grazed his teeth against her lips, lingered, then slowly, his tongue entered her mouth and the passion between them ignited.

"Come to bed", said Jasmine as she led him up the stairs.

Their clothes found their resting place on the floor. Leo's breath was hot and quickening as he laid his body on top of Jasmine's quivering and excited flesh. His tongue tangled with hers in a battle for passionate dominance. He lowered himself gently, his lips explored her neck and throat. She felt his hot breath on her breasts. Jasmine wrapped her legs around him as he thrusted his hardness deep into her.

"Oh Gawd", they both moaned as their pleasure erupted simultaneously.

They both lay in silence side by side, exhausted from their passionate reunion. Leo was also exhausted from travelling and Jasmine, from the grief of losing her dear friend and the day's events. They both drifted off slowly to sleep in each other's arms.

Jasmine awoke first. She turned on her side and rested her head on her hand, supported by her elbow. She watched Leo sleeping. He looked so beautiful. She gently, without touching, drew her finger around the outline of his jaw.

"What are you doing", said Leo, as he opened one eye.

"I wanted to touch you to make sure you were real, but didn't want to wake you", she replied.

With that he rolled over gently on top of her, kissed her and made love to her again.....and again.

They spent the day relaxing at Jasmine's house. Leo briefly met Alex at the breakfast table. Alex said, "Hiya butt", shook his hand then grabbed a piece of toast, kissed his mum, then said,

"See you again butt", as he went off with his guitar case tucked under his arm to meet his university band mates for a practice session in his friend's garage.

"Man of many words", laughed Leo.

"I think he's a bit embarrassed", said Jasmine.

"So when do you go back?" she asked.

"Oh, right, want rid of me already do you?" asked Leo cheekily.

"No you daft bugger. I just want to know how much time we have together".

"I fly out early hours of tomorrow, but I wish I could stay longer".

"Stay", pleaded Jasmine.

"I wish I could. I have to go back for work. But I'll see you soon, right?" He queried.

Jasmine looked bemused.

"What? When?"

"Didn't Steph say anything?"

"About what?" asked Jasmine.

"Did she give you anything after the funeral?" said Leo, fearing he had said something he shouldn't have.

"Noooo, what are you talking about? Oh wait, Steve gave me an envelope just before we left the pub."

She pulled the crumpled up envelope from her bag. Her intention was to read it when she got home, but with Leo arriving unexpectedly, it went clean out of her mind.

She opened it cautiously. Leo examined her face as he sipped his coffee.

She read the letter that was inside the envelope out loud. Teardrops trickled from the corners of her eyes. It was from Cerys.

"My dearest friend. I am so sorry I didn't tell you how ill I was. I couldn't bear to see you sad. I wanted my last few weeks to be filled with fun, happiness and joy and thanks to you it was. I love you mate. I won't deny that I am shit scared of the unknown. I hope it will be peaceful where ever I go. I have had enough raving, partying and debauchery to last anyone's life time. I have loved every waking minute, every woman I have been with...including you...but didn't fancy you in that way, as sexy and gorgeous as you are, you're more like a sister...not a 'scissor one' either before you comment. You knew that though...wink wink.

I hope you have made it up with Leo".

He grabbed her hand as she read on with a trembling voice.

"He is a great guy. He is honest and truly likes you. I vetted him good and proper, you know me, and in my line of work, it was second nature".

Leo nodded and smiled. Jasmine continued to read. She wiped the tears away. Her cheeks were warm from blushing.

"I made sure he wasn't going to mess you about or rip your heart out. He really does like you mate, and I mean 'REALLY' like you. Not just out of pity or any of that crap. I spoke to him the other day, (before I popped off that is...you shouldn't be reading this yet if I haven't)... and warned him. If he pisses you off in any way shape or form I will haunt the bastard until the day he dies.

Anyway, as you can tell by my hand writing, I'm getting a bit tired now, so before I go, I have one last thing to give you. In the other envelope attached to the back of this essay, there is a cheque for you along with that (crappy)...only messing... beautiful necklace you bought me. You have got to go back to Hawaii for the Pearl Harbour Remembrance day ceremony where you will be able to see Leo in his Marine uniform...woof woof! There is enough there for you to have a good few days there my love. This is my final wish for you to go...so bloody well go...or I'll haunt you too! I have squared it with your Sergeant at work so there is no excuse. Keep my necklace as a reminder of the fantastic holiday we had. Well I have to go, the devil is calling me.

Enjoy Hawaii... AGAIN! I will watch over you...that sounds creepy doesn't it... GOOD!

P.S Please can you post the letter addressed to Louisa, (you know that bit of stuff I met on our way out to Hawaii), that's in the envelope with your cheque. I didn't want Steph and our dad to see it....got to keep some secrets eh! I wanted to tell her just in case she tried to get in touch with me...that would be awkward wouldn't it!

Good bye my beautiful friend.

Cerys

xxxxxx "

Jasmine was crying uncontrollably by the time she finished reading the letter. Leo had watery eyes too. He held her closely, stroking her hair and rocking her in his arms.

"I miss her so much Leo".

"Shhhhh, I know, it's okay", he whispered, "It's okay".

Jasmine opened the envelope with the cheque in and the letter to Louisa, when Leo was in the shower. He was going to discuss the plans that Cerys had made with him, afterwards.

The necklace fell to the floor. She picked it up quickly and attached it to her very same necklace that she was wearing. She pressed her hand against it as she read the cheque. It was for five thousand pounds. She couldn't believe it. She felt guilty, surprised, startled. Why had her friend given her so much? She wanted to give it back to Steph. She couldn't take it. She rang Steph immediately.

"Steph, its Jas, how are you?"

"Not good, how are you?"

"The same. It's great having Leo here though. He has been a great comfort".

"I was so pleased when you told me, honestly Jas, I couldn't have wished for anything better...except to have Cerys back".

"I know.... Umm...this is awkward....the cheque... I can't take it, I really can't. It's yours.

I will post it back to you later, okay. I can't take it Steph".

"Don't you bloody dare! I will be really offended if you do. Please, you have to go to Hawaii again, please love. Cerys wanted it. We have enough insurance policies and her Police federation cover to last my lifetime. She made sure we were all taken care of, don't you worry."

"Okay, but it just doesn't feel right", said Jasmine.

"It will. Now listen, go back to Leo, enjoy your time with him. I won't be jetting off with work for a while yet so please come and see me and keep me updated with everything okay? Don't forget to post that letter to Louisa too?"

"You know about that?" asked Jasmine.

"Yep. She fell asleep as she was writing it. It dropped on the floor so I picked it up and read a little bit of it. I put it back without her noticing. I'm fine about it. That's the type of relationship we had. I just think she didn't want to hurt me, her being ill when it happened and all. I will always love her Jas".

"I know you will. I will see you soon Steph.....and thank you. I will have to dig out my bikini again. Take care".

"Someone mention bikinis", said Leo as he emerged from the bathroom with his towel wrapped around his waist.

"Oh my", replied Jasmine as she looked him up and down hungrily.

She watched him as he dressed himself, biting her bottom lip as he zipped up his jeans.

They went and bought fish and chips for lunch after they had taken Ruby out for a little walk. Leo wanted to see the sights of the little Welsh Village where Jasmine lived. Later they snuggled up in front of the log burner discussing their plans for their 'Hawaii -part two' trip. It was too cloudy, gloomy and cold to go anywhere else.

"Okay, me and the guys and gals, the cast and crew, will arrive late evening on the 5th December for rehearsals and stuff so if you can get a flight to arrive on the 6th December that would be perfect. I have a hotel room booked already so you can stay with me."

Jasmine nodded intently. They were sat either end of the settee with their legs entwined.

"Let me know as soon as you have booked it, times etc. and I will meet you at the airport. I will get you a good spot so you can see the President and the speeches. I won't be able to stand with you as I will be with the cast from the show and we will all be dressed in out uniforms commemorating the real characters we played. It's gonna be emotional... I'll tell ya".

"OOOh... then what happens after?" asked Jasmine.

"Well, bring your dancing shoes as there will be a party to go to afterwards...all 1940s style. I won't be chucking you around doing a jive though right?"

"Are you saying I'm too heavy", Jasmine gently kicked him.

"No, not at all, it's me, I can't do all that stuff, I'll either drop you or kill you!" he laughed.

"Well we had better stick to the dances where both out feet stay on the floor then", chuckled Jasmine.

The time flew by quickly and Leo had to leave for the airport. Jasmine insisted on driving him even though she had to be in work early the next day. She wouldn't be able to sleep anyway. Everything that had happened in the last few weeks, and now the sudden plans to go back to Hawaii had left her mind reeling.

He loved his trip in a tiny mini called Lilliputia, winding along country lanes, swerving to avoid potholes. He held on tightly to the safety bar most of the way and teased Jasmine about her driving techniques.

She waved him off at the gate at the airport after a long lingering kiss, smiling to herself as she drove home, touching her lips occasionally, remembering Leo's touch.

"Hmmmmm".

Chapter 27

Jasmine's plane landed at Honolulu airport. It had been a long flight on her own and quite sad as the last time she went she was with Cerys. She wanted to talk to her so badly.

"Aloha, welcome to Hawaii" said the airport staff as they placed a couple of colourful leis over her head and arranged it around her shoulders. Jasmine was dressed in a knee length, belted, capped sleeved, round neck, turquoise dress and cream pumps. She adjusted and smoothed down the skirt of her dress and checked it hadn't been eaten by her underwear. The sun was warm but the sky was slightly cloudier. It was definitely a lot cooler than when she was there a few weeks before. The familiar scent of the Hawaiian flora hung on the light breeze, just as she remembered. She pressed the palm of her hand on the doubled up turtle necklaces that she had bought for her and Cerys.

"Hope you are with me babe", she whispered to herself.

The airport was decorated with flags and World War Two memorabilia. The musical sound of The Glen Miller band echoed in the background of the busy airport. She had landed in 1941!

Jasmine scanned the faces of the crowd of people who had come to collect their friends and relatives. She searched for Leo desperately.

She could see a sign which was held up high above the heads of a group of army cadets, and on it was written,

"Over here Jasmine, your carriage awaits".

Leo pushed his way through a group of army cadets and Jasmine ran towards him. He was wearing knee length denim shorts and a white t-shirt with his sun glasses clipped on the neckline. He dropped the sign, picked her up and swung her around, kissing her passionately, accidentally causing her to kick a few travellers in the knees as her out of control feet left the ground.

"Let's get you out of here", grinned Leo.

He grabbed her case and she slung her handbag over her shoulder. He held her hand tightly as he guided her out of the buzzing airport.

"Your chariot", said Leo as he pointed out a clapped out old army jeep without a roof.

"I borrowed it from the crew's props. They won't mind. I tried to hire a car but it was impossible. The Island is overrun with people attending for the Anniversary. Hang on tightly".

"Jeez, and you had the cheek to take the piss out of my driving? For a start you drive on the wrong side of the road and you drive like a ninety year old lady", shouted Jasmine over the loud noise of the open top, clattering old jeep.

"We stick to the speed limit around here and I think it would fall to pieces if I tried to go any faster anyways", he shouted back.

After a bumpy and dusty ride they arrived at the hotel. It was quite basic compared to the Turtle Bay Resort that they had both stayed at last time, but it was enough for them. It was on the fifth floor so they had to either climb the staircase or squeeze into a small lift. They opted for the lift as it was no hardship for them having to press their bodies close together. There was a double bed, a bathroom that had a shower a loo and a basin, one arm chair in the room, a small rail to hang clothes, a T.V and a complimentary coffee making set. There wasn't a balcony, just a very large window that faced towards another hotel nearby.

Leo's clothes were already hanging up. Jasmine unpacked hers and hung them up next to his leaving her undies and shoes and other items in the case. He laid on the bed with his hands behind his neck, watching her every move.

"I have to go and meet the cast and crew in about two hours, sorry I'll have to leave you for a bit, is that okay?"

"Oh great, so I travel all this way and you abandon me", said Jasmine as she flicked him with a towel.

"I know, but I'm all yours after the ceremony, I promise"

"Alright then. I am a bit knackered I must admit. I'll rest here and conserve my energy for when you return", she giggled as she crawled between his legs and laid on top of him.

"How about we go for some chow before I go? I know great place a few blocks away" he said as he smacked and grabbed her backside and pulled her up closer to him.

"Sounds like a plan Skipper", she said as she kissed him lightly, "but I need a shower first as I stink".

"Yes you do", he laughed. She pressed her armpit against his face to make him suffer for his comment. He jokingly mouthed. "Phew", before pushing her arm away.

"Care to join me?" she winked as she climbed off him and wiggled her way to the bathroom.

Clothes strewn all over the bathroom floor, steam rolled out of the shower stall and crept over the mirror leaving streaks as it dripped. The sound of giggles gradually turned to moans of pleasure as Leo and Jasmine unleashed their lust for one another once again.

Hair dripping wet, she rubbed it as best as she could with a towel, Jasmine scraped it back off her face into a bun. She changed her travel clothes for shorts and a t-shirt. Leo put on the clothes he had dropped on the bathroom floor. They walked hand in hand to a bar and grill which was one block from the waterfront. They were both ravenous after their adventurous shower so they ordered large grilled chicken breast sandwiches with fries, with a large glass of ice cold beer.

"So what do you call me when you tell your mates about me then?" asked Jasmine whilst chewing her burger and covering her mouth with one hand so Leo didn't see the contents.

"Uhhh...Jasmine...that's your name right?"

"No you daft bugger....am I your sweetheart or your lover?" she grinned.

"Ummm...shut up and eat your food. I'm a guy, we don't say stuff like that", he laughed.

He walked her back to the hotel before leaving her to go for his rehearsal. They bought a bottle of wine from a liquor store on the way so that she could have a glass whilst she waited for him to come back to her.

Chapter 28

Jasmine was awoken by Leo climbing into bed with her. She had dozed off after one glass of wine and the gentle hum of the air conditioning helped her to relax. She was shattered after her long distance journey and she still hadn't fully gained her strength after losing her friend.

His chest was pressed against her back and he nestled his chin into her neck whilst wrapping his arm around her waist, pulling himself tight up against her. He kissed her neck and within seconds he was out for the count.

They were awoken early by Leo's alarm on his mobile phone.

"Morning gorgeous, sleep well?" he asked as he tried to pull the duvet away from Jasmine. She was clinging onto it tightly.

"Five more minutes, don't you know the rules about waking up a sleeping woman? You should only do so if it's snowing or if a celebrity has died", she whispered from her slumber.

"Now c'mon we have to get moving. He turned her over onto her back and pulled her legs down the bed towards him. He was stood at the bottom of the bed by now. He attempted to tickle her feet but she went to kick him in the balls so he thought better of it.

"Okay... five more minutes whilst I grab a shower...then when you take a shower I will go and get us a takeout breakfast, bring it here and we can eat it before we get going... yeah?"

"Yeah...my my, last of the big spenders eh!" mumbled Jasmine as she pulled the duvet back over her head.

"Tomorrow, I will take you for a proper American breakfast, but we don't have time today", he said quite sternly as he climbed into the shower.

"Yes sir", Jasmine replied with a salute as she peeked over the top of her duvet.

She was showered, dressed and ready to go when Leo arrived back with large coffees, fresh fruit and pancakes in takeaway cartons.

"You look darn pretty", said Leo as he admired Jasmine's efforts to dress in a 1940's outfit which she had bought from a vintage clothing shop in Cardiff. She had styled her hair with her curling wand into a classic Rita Hayworth look. She had bright red lipstick to enhance her style.

"Well thank you. I can't wait to see you in your uniform."

"I have got this for you to wear though", said Leo as he pulled out a 1940s nurses uniform.

"You can wear your dress to the party later. I got you this so you can mix in with the cast and you will be right at the front of the ceremony, not far from me. Only if you want too."

"Oh Gawd, I dunno. Will I have to do anything or say anything? Am I allowed to do that?" replied Jasmine hesitantly.

"I spoke to the producer and the other cast members and they said it was a great idea, so some of the girls sneaked a spare outfit out of the costume department. You will be able to honour the nurses that sacrificed their lives too. You won't have to utter a word, just stand there looking proud and smart. What da ya think?"

"Oh shit...oh go on then" said Jasmine as she admired the full dress parade uniform and not the actual white dress and apron she imagined.

She put on the shirt and skirt, tie and jacket. Leo pulled out some stockings from the pocket of the jacket.

"Let me see you put these babies on" he grinned.

He proceeded to get dressed after drooling at the sight of Jasmine seductively rolling her stocking up to her thighs.

He wore the full dress kit as well, not the battle kit. The producers and directors of the series had asked the families of the fallen soldiers which uniform they would like the actors to wear in their honour and they all chose the full dress uniform. The surviving twenty four Pearl Harbour veterans were also going to wear the same.

"Can't wait to take them back off you", he winked.

Both stood in front of the mirror in the bathroom, fully dressed in their uniforms, putting their caps on. Jasmine had rolled her hair up and pinned it into a top knot, so that she would look the part.

Leo wolf whistled as Jasmine did a twirl in front of him.

"Does my bum look big in this?" She asked.

"Never", he replied.

"You look pretty damn sexy too, if you don't mind me saying", she whispered in his ear.

"You 'say- away' hot stuff", he replied.

Leo grabbed his phone and took a picture of them both.

"Ready?" Leo asked.

"Ready, I think", Jasmine replied.

"Oh, I almost forgot, passes to get in", said Leo as he handed Jasmine an entrance pass.

All the flags were flying at half-staff as Leo and Jasmine drove to the site that overlooks where the USS Arizona sank. They remained like that until sunset.

"Does this jeep sound okay to you?" asked Jasmine. "I can hear knocking or ticking or something, and it smells of oil or something".

"I'm not sure, the engine is so darn noisy, and old, it's hard to tell. It's not far to go if we break down", replied Leo.

Everywhere was decorated like it was the 1940s. People were dressed up, and again the sound of big band music could be heard in the background. They followed the road signs for organisers, guests, cast and crew. Leo parked the jeep near to an area designated for prop and set vehicles. He graciously held Jasmine around the waist as he led her to a seating and standing area near a raised platform.

"Hey Skipper, over here".

Joe, Dylan and Rick waved as Leo and Jasmine walked towards them.

"Well hello beautiful", said Joe as he eyed Jasmine up and down and kissed the back of her hand.

"You remember these guys?" said Leo.

"Of course, how could I forget these handsome fellas", smiled Jasmine.

"Hey Jasmine, you are looking mighty fine in that uniform, are you sure Leo is the man for you?" said Rick.

"Hey, lay off her, she is with me." said Leo as he slipped his hand around her waist and pulled her close in to him.

"I'm gonna bag a dance with you later gal", winked Dylan.

"Ignore him, I will not let you out of my sight. Let me take over to the cast of nurses."

He led her away to a group of about twenty women actors all dressed up in their nurses' parade uniforms too.

"I will leave you in the capable hands of Julia and Rainbow.

I'll just be over there with the guys. We'll grab some lunch after the ceremony, then have a rest before the celebration party, is that good for you?"

"Sounds fab. See ya later skipper".

"Hi I'm Jasmine, I hope you are expecting me otherwise I'm going to feel pretty daft if you weren't", she said as she offered a hand shake to Julia and Rainbow.

"Hello, of course we were expecting you. Leo has filled us in. He is pretty romantic right? Travelling to England to see you and all. Sorry about your friend by the way", said Rainbow in a real southern drawl.

"It's Wales by the way not England. Where are you from Rainbow, and I must say, what a wonderful name?"

"Why, I'm sorry ma'am, I get confused with my countries. I'm from Dallas and my parents were hippies". She rolled her eyes and grinned. "Julia here is from New York. We have been actors off and on for about ten years Julia, right?" she asked.

"Yeah, about that. Oh shoot, we had better get lined up. Stand between us, can I call you Jas?"

"Yes of course" replied Jasmine.

"I love your accent, so cute and lyrical. Would love to chat to you more after. Any-hoo, all we have to do is salute when they call and mention the nursing army corps we are here to represent okay. This is how we do it".

Julia proceeded to show Jasmine how to salute with Leo watching on fondly. Everyone lined up. Actors in one section with a banner behind them with "1941 - 1945" written on it, and the real, current military and medical corps in another section. Honoured guests and veterans, who were proudly and deservedly wearing their medals, were ushered to the seating area at the front of the raised platform. The public then followed on and watched from behind barriers and the Guard of Honour, Military Police, Honolulu Police and Special Forces surrounded the venue.

The sound of a helicopter filled the air and within minutes the Presidential cavalcade of limousines hurtled forward towards the side of the raised platform. Groups of Special Force Body guards and Military Personnel surrounded the second car. The President emerged, waving at the crowd as he walked towards the raised platform, still surrounded by his body guards. He walked towards the microphone and the murmuring of the crowd came to complete silence. The Marine band played, 'The Presidential March' as he arrived in position.

He honoured and welcomed the military, the guests, veterans, dignitary and all the crowd who had attended to remember the fallen and their families. He also honoured the twenty four surviving Pearl Harbour Veterans. He went on to mention the actors who portrayed real life characters who played their role in the Second World War.

"Stop fidgeting", whispered Rainbow to Jasmine who was feeling hot and uncomfortable in her uniform.

She felt a bit excited and wanted to control the voice in her head that wanted to shout out,

"Look it's the President of the United States", but she managed to contain herself.

She looked across to Leo who was directly opposite her. He looked drop dead gorgeous and made her tingle all the way down to her naughty bits. She could feel her ovaries popping one by one. She came to her senses and tried to look away, feeling that it was highly inappropriate to feel like this at such an event. He watched her intently.

The President announced that the cast from various War TV Series and films would represent and honour their characters, real soldiers, they portrayed with the blessing of their families.

The actor who played Sgt John Basilone stepped forward from his line.

"John Basilone was a United States Marine Gunnery Sergeant who received the nation's highest military award for valour, the Medal of Honour, for heroism during the Battle of Guadalcanal in World War II. He was the only Marine enlisted man to receive both the Medal of Honour and the Navy Cross in World War II. God Bless you Sgt Basilone."

The actor saluted and stepped back into line.

The next actor stepped forward. He played Private Eugene Sledge.

"Once he was out of school, Eugene Sledge was assigned duty as an enlisted man and was eventually assigned to K (King) Company, 3rd Battalion, 5th Marines, 1st Marine Division (K/3/5). He achieved the rank of Private First Class in the war of the Pacific and saw combat as a 60mm mortar man at Peleliu and Okinawa. When fighting grew too close for effective use of the mortar he served in other duties such as stretcher bearer and providing rifle fire. During his service, Sledge kept notes of what happened in his pocket sized New Testament. When the war ended, he took these notes and compiled them into the memoir that was to be known as With the Old Breed. I salute you Private Sledge".

The actor saluted and stepped back.

Next was the actor who played US Marine Robert Leckie.

"On January 18, 1942, Leckie enlisted in the United States Marine Corps. He served in combat in the Battle of the Pacific, as a scout and a machine gunner in H Company, 2nd Battalion, 1st Marine Regiment, 1st Marine Division. Leckie saw combat in the Battle of Guadalcanal, the Battle of Cape Gloucester, and had been wounded by blast concussion in the Battle of Peleliu. Due to his wounds, he was evacuated to an Army field hospital on the Pavuvu Islands. He returned to the United States in March 1945 and was honourably discharged shortly thereafter. He wrote a book, his war memoirs called "A helmet for my pillow". I salute you Robert Leckie.

Then Leo stepped forward. Jasmine's heart skipped a few beats. He hadn't told her he was doing this. She knew he had been carrying out rehearsals but he wouldn't divulge what for or what he would be doing. She sneaked a smile as he glanced at her.

"Captain Andrew Haldane, Ack Ack as he was nicknamed, became a second lieutenant in the Marine Corps in 1942, graduating from the Reserve Officers' Training School in Quantico. He served with the 1st Marine Division on Guadalcanal and was commanding officer of Company K at Cape Gloucester, where he received the Silver Star for leading hand-to-hand combat in a fight on Walt's Ridge. He led Company K through most of the fight for Peleliu. Haldane was shot by a Japanese sniper on October 12, 1944, while assessing the area of Hill 140 during the Battle of Peleliu in the Palau Islands, three days before the Marines came off the lines. A Sea Scouts Ship was named in his honour at his old college. I salute you Captain Haldane".

Jasmine quivered from head to toe. She felt so proud of him.

Some of the Cast of the series, "Band of Brothers", stepped forward to represent their characters along with some of the cast of the film of "Saving Private Ryan", "Wind talkers" and various other productions that represented the bravery of the fallen and their families.

The President also mentioned the cast who represented the decorated Medical and Nursing Corps. Julia nudged Jasmine to salute. She managed to do it in time and correctly. Leo gave her a sneaky thumbs up.

The President thanked them all and went on to make his statement.

"Seventy years ago today, a bright Sunday morning was darkened by the unprovoked attack on Pearl Harbour. Today, Michelle and I join the American people in honouring the memory of the more than two thousand, four hundred American patriots, military and civilian, men, women and children, who gave their lives in our first battle of the Second World War. Our thoughts and prayers are with the families for whom this day is deeply personal, the spouses, brothers and sisters, and sons and daughters who have known seven decades without a loved one but who have kept their legacy alive for future generations. We salute the veterans and survivors of Pearl Harbour who inspire us still. Despite overwhelming odds, they fought back heroically, inspiring our nation and putting us on the path to victory. They are members of that Greatest Generation who overcame the Depression, crossed oceans and stormed the beaches to defeat fascism, and turned adversaries into our closest allies. When the guns fell silent, they came home, went to school on the G.I. Bill, and built the largest middle class in history and the strongest economy in the world. They remind us that no challenge is too great when Americans stand as one. All of us owe these men and women a profound debt of gratitude for the freedoms and standard of living we enjoy today.

On this National Pearl Harbour Remembrance Day, we also reaffirm our commitment to carrying on their work, to keeping the country we love strong, free and prosperous. And as today's wars in Iraq and Afghanistan come to an end and we welcome home our 9/11 Generation, we resolve to always take care of our troops, veterans and military families as well as they've taken care of us. On this solemn anniversary, there can be no higher tribute to the Americans who served and sacrificed seventy years ago today."

There was a loud explosion that immediately drowned out the President. There was smoke and flames in the distance near to the props car park where Leo had parked his jeep. People screamed and ducked. The group of body guards surrounded the President whilst another group of Special Agents and armed Marines ran towards the commotion. Soldiers and Naval staff circled the crowd and attempted to calm them down.

The casting directors had told the acting cast to remain in line where they were, not to worry the crowd. Jasmine gripped the sides of her uniform jacket with fear as she desperately searched for Leo. She couldn't see him or a couple of the other actors he was stood next too.

"Where's Leo?" she urgently asked Rainbow.

"Don't worry. One of the crew tapped him on the shoulder after the explosion. He and few of the other guys walked off behind the platform with the crew. He'll be back soon, don't worry. We'll take care of you."

A rush of security and Special agents dashed back towards the President. They whispered something to him, he nodded and took hold of the microphone.

"Everyone, no need to be alarmed. My trusted security have informed me the explosion was nothing but an electrical fault with one of the props. I'm so sorry. Please settle down and we'll continue with the ceremony."

One of the Marine band members rushed towards the platform and one of the guards bent down to speak to him. The guard then whispered to the President. Again he spoke with the microphone.

"Sorry folks, before we continue with the two minute silence, I have an unusual request, can anyone play the bugle? Our bugler from the Marine band has fallen ill and it wouldn't seem natural not to have the Last Post played at such an important military event."

The crowd mumbled and muttered amongst themselves, looking around to see if anyone would step forward.

Jasmine looked at Rainbow then at Julia. Her face was all red and hot.

She stepped forward.

"What are you doing?" whispered Julia as she tried to pull her back by the bottom of her skirt.

Jasmine held up her hand like she did when she was in school to ask the teacher a question.

"Umm, hello, excuse me", she said in a tiny mouse like squeal. "Excuse me sir. I used to play the bugle many years ago when I was in Sea Cadets."

"The Sea what? Never mind, officer, go and bring her to the platform", said the President to the Marine that had approached him.

The crowd whispered and wondered amongst themselves.

With that a Marine marched over towards her and ushered her over to the band on the side of the platform. He passed her the bugle. She wiped the mouth piece with her sleeve, looked back at the band who all appeared to look extremely worried. The Marine told her he would nod when she had to play it.

The two minute silence began. All she could think of was,

"Shit shit shit breathe shit shit shit". She searched for Leo again. He was back in line with the others, watching her like a worried parent, chewing anxiously on his bottom lip. With a deep breath, she lifted the bugle to her lips, eyes glued on the Marine. There was a sharp intake of breath from the band and the crowd. The President watched her with wide and inquisitive eyes. The nod came, she shut her eyes tightly and played 'The Last Post 'in front of President Obama, only the President of the United States of America, only one of the most powerful men in the world....and she played it in front of Leo.

The first note was a bit wobbly but she played the rest of it elegantly. She put the bugle down by her side when she had finished. The sweat bubbled and glistened on her top lip and brow. She took a deep breath and looked up at the President. He nodded back at her.

Leo and the others were grinning like Cheshire Cats, so she rolled her eyes and grinned back. She almost jumped out of her skin when the band stood up behind her to play, "The Star Spangled Banner". She placed her hand on her heart, copying everyone else, and mouthed the words as best as she could.

After the President thanked everyone and waved as he left the platform, his security guards surrounded him as he moved from the platform. The Marine who was stood by the side of Jasmine told her to remain where she was until the President had left. The security guards stopped in front of her and they parted. The President stepped forward like Moses walking through the Red Sea and offered Jasmine a hand shake.

"Thank you for stepping in ma'am. What is your name and where are you from?"

She bowed, curtsied and saluted all in one go.

"No need for that", he said.

"I'm Jasmine from Wales Sir, in Britain. I'm with him, over by there." she replied nervously pointing towards Leo. The President turned to look at him.

"Sorry Sir, I'm here on holiday, vacation you call it, and my friend is an actor and asked me to be part of this. It was a great honour and privilege to meet you sir". She spoke so quickly and over extenuated her accent, she could tell by the look on his face that he had no idea what she had said. He also shrugged his shoulders as he looked at his body guards.

"Well thank you Jasmine, enjoy your time here". He went on to shake hands with the veterans and dignitary before getting into his limo and heading back off to his helicopter.

The military led the seated people out first, then the crowd and then allowed the actors to disperse.

Jasmine ran straight towards Leo, one stocking rolling down slowly as she did. She jumped into his arms, the other actors clapped as she did.

"Wow, you are full of tricks", laughed Leo.

"I need to pee badly. I almost did it in front of the President." she winced.

"C'mon" he said as he led her towards the loos.

"I have to have a debrief with the crew then I'll be done. Wait here when you are done okay. It won't take long," said Leo.

"Hey, where did you go after that loud bang before?" She asked just before she opened the loo door.

"I'll tell you later", he said as he walked towards the other actors.

Chapter 29

Jasmine waited patiently near to the loos for Leo to meet her. She paced up and down, adjusted her collar on her shirt a few times with her finger and adjusted her stockings as she was feeling quite hot and uncomfortable.

"Ready?" said Leo, quite out of breath as he jogged towards her.

"Where have you been? Can we go back to the hotel and change in to something more comfortable now?" whined Jasmine.

Leo looked ashen and his expression was deadly serious.

"No problem, but we will have to get a cab", he said as he took hold of her hand and led her out of the compound.

"Where's the jeep?" asked Jasmine

"Um, well... you know that explosion before? That was our jeep", said Leo nervously removing his cap and rubbing his neck.

"What do you mean? Shit...faulty electrics was it? We were lucky, we could have been toast", exclaimed Jasmine as she trotted along behind Leo. He seemed to be quickening his pace as they walked and this made her stockings roll down even quicker.

"Stop...stop. My stockings are rolling down and my drawers will be falling down next if you don't slow down," she shouted... "What's the matter?"

"Let's grab a cab and I will explain back at the hotel, right"?

The cab ride back to the hotel room was silent. Leo seemed distant and his eyes stared straight ahead as if they were willing for the journey to be over quickly. Jasmine squeezed his hand tightly to remind him she was there but he didn't respond back.

As they arrived at the hotel, a Police car was waiting for them and Leo appeared to have been expecting them. He told Jasmine to go on up to the room and get changed and he would be up shortly. He stayed in the lobby speaking with the Police Officers.

Jasmine was beside herself with worry. She took off the uniform and folded it up neatly. She threw the stockings across the room in temper because they annoyed her and were damn uncomfortable and also because she didn't have a clue what Leo was doing. She sat on the edge of the bed in her underwear thinking all sorts of horror stories.

Was Leo in trouble for taking the jeep that wasn't road worthy?

Was he in trouble because it exploded near to the President?

Did the police think he caused the explosion to kill the President?

She felt dizzy and sick with worry. As she was pulling on a t-shirt and shorts Leo came into the room and sat on the edge of the bed. He kicked his boots off and placed his head in his hands.

"Jasmine, I'm so sorry".

Jasmine stood frozen to the spot. Her faced felt flushed and hot and her stomach was in knots.

She swallowed hard before saying,

"Sorry for what? What have you done"?

He looked up at her. His eyes were red and his worry lines were deepened. He took hold of her hand and pulled her towards him. She stood in front of him, staring hard.

"Tell me, what is it?"

"In the debrief the one of the security guards told us that the jeep was rigged with an amateur bomb device. The Police have just told me in the lobby that there was a timing device on it and they believe it was supposed to go off when we left the hotel to go to the memorial service this morning, but thankfully it was faulty and didn't work. At the ceremony, we all thought it was the electrics that caused it to explode, being so old and all. We saw the smoke coming from the direction of the jeep so that's why we left for a short time to check it out. The marine that was supposed to play the bugle hadn't fallen ill, he didn't turn up for the ceremony. He was found tied up and gagged in a nearby truck. He was on his way to the ceremony and saw a kid, a teenager, messing around under the hood of the jeep. He went over to him to ask him what he was doing and the kid punched him in the face and hit him with a wrench, then dragged him to a truck and tied him up.

The kid ran when he saw the Presidents vehicles approaching the site but one of the security guys saw him, thought he was suspicious and chased him for quite a while."

Jasmine sat down next to him on the bed and placed on hand on his shoulder.

"Go on", she said.

"The security guy finally managed to catch him and haul his ass back to the site but just as they arrived the jeep exploded. The kid was bundled off in a police van and questioned at the police station. When they searched him they found a photograph of me and you and a letter written in German from a prison on the mainland. The kid was Astrid's brother. She had offered him a substantial amount of money to come to Hawaii to kill us. She knew that I was coming back for the memorial service and guessed that you would be here too. The kid cracked straight away. It didn't take much for him to break down. He's only eighteen years old for Christ's sake. What's the matter with her?"

Jasmine didn't know what to say. She took a deep breath and shouted,

"What the hell......"

"I know, I know babe, come here. I'm so sorry that you are involved in all of this......and to think", he gulped, "I could have got you killed, I couldn't live with myself. So, maybe.....maybe we should call it quits and go and live our separate lives. I can't risk it anymore"

He let go of her hand stood up and walked towards the window, tears rolling down his face.

Jasmine walked towards him and wrapped her arms around his waist and buried her head into his back. He pushed her away with one arm, not aggressively but enough to make her jump.

"Leo, c'mon. We are alive, and we are alright. The kid messed up and was caught and no doubt Astrid will suffer serious consequences because of this. We'll be okay, c'mon".

Leo wouldn't turn around. She tried to turn him around and pull his face to hers but he pulled back and stood like stone staring out of the window.

Jasmine stepped backwards slowly, rubbing her arm that he had pushed, the familiar feeling of fear, rejection and uncertainty had reared its ugly head yet again. She ran to the bathroom and slammed the door. She slumped down on the floor against the door. She couldn't cry. She had no more tears left, none what so ever. She felt numb. The mood of the day had gone from the highest to the lowest possible point in a matter of moments.

After a few minutes she heard the door of the hotel room slam. She pulled herself up and slowly opened the bathroom door.

"Leo......Leo", she called out. There was no answer.

His clothes and items had gone. Her neatly folded up uniform had also gone except for one stocking which was loosely hanging from the air conditioning controls.

"Bastard", she shouted out at the top of her lungs. She couldn't believe he would give up so easily. 'Maybe this was his way of dumping her, an easy way out, use all this as an excuse. He had done what Cerys had asked and now it was time for him to move on', she thought to herself.

She sat for a while wondering what the hell had just happened and what the hell she was going to do now. She still had two more days left of her stay there.

She picked up her phone to text Steph but stopped herself. Steph didn't need this on top of everything else.

"Bugger it", she thought. She tidied herself up and took herself out for a liquid lunch followed by a stroll on the beach.

Several martinis and Mai Tais later, she sat on the beach and watched families and friend's having fun. She felt so ineffably lonely. She wrote "Cerys" over and over again in the sand with a small pebble and, "all men are pigs" underneath. A white feather blew in the breeze and rested on her foot.

"Feathers appear when angels are near," she quoted and whispered under her breath, "Hey Cerys, I knew you would make it to angel status. I need you mate". She stroked the feather gently with the tips of her fingers.

A figure stood in front and over her. She shaded her eyes to see who it was but the sun blackened them out.

"Not all men sweetheart", laughed the man standing over her. "I have been searching all over for you".

"And who...whom...who....may I ask is calling," replied Jasmine tipsily.

The man held his hand out to help her up. It was Rick, one of Leo's actor friends.

"Why have you....yes you....been looking for me? You know that bastard has fucked off and abandoned me, do ya, do ya?" she said slurring and waving her finger uncontrollably at him.

"Come on, I think you need some coffee and chow", said Rick as he gripped Jasmine's elbow to help her along.

"Don't you touch me", she said angrily, "Just don't, okay".

Rick thought this was highly amusing and held his hands up in surrender and then had to cover his smirk with one hand as he followed her closely from behind.

He guided her into a diner and ordered them both coffee and a BLT.

"So why on earth have you been looking for me?" asked Jasmine, gulping back her coffee.

"Well, my buddy Leo feels like shit right now. He is just as, or perhaps maybe more, wasted than you. He is in my hotel room crying like a big girl snuggled up to a whiskey bottle. So this is what I have done. I have been to the police station and spoken to the cops myself to find out what the hell has been going on. I was with Leo last time, after the Halloween parade, when the cops spoke to us, so they knew I was part of Leo's group from then, so were happy to divulge the information. That Astrid bitch… all that stuff is over. The prison have checked all her correspondence and it seems as if the only person she has ever contacted from the slammer is her brother, Lukas.

The parents have washed their hands of Astrid as she has been in and out of trouble for years. Lukas is a bright kid but it seems his much older sister is a bit of a control freak and he is frightened of her. She threatened him with all sorts if he didn't follow her instructions to blow you both up. He will be deported back to Germany and dealt with there by the authorities. His parents are fully aware of all that has happened and they are horrified. So, she can't get to you anymore. I've told Leo this but he is too terrified to show his feelings again as he feels as though he has put you in danger too many times Jas. He is besotted with you."

Jasmine shrugged her shoulders.

"Did he send you?"

"No, he doesn't know I'm here".

"So"? She said coquettishly.

"So missy, here's what we are gonna do. You are gonna go and get cleaned up and changed and I will pick you up from your hotel around eight o'clock and take you to a 1940s party. The guys and gals that were at the actors' reunion today, will be there, including Leo if I can drag him off that whiskey bottle. We'll have a blast and put all this crap behind us. You two were meant to be together. Jeez, I sound like something from a woman's magazine don't I".

"No, I don't think so. My heart can't take another kicking to be honest. Thanks for lunch and all and tell Leo to have a nice life," Jasmine said coldly as she stood up, still a bit tipsy and unsteady, slapping a handful of dollars on the table as she went.

Rick paid the waitress for and lunch quickly and ran after her and shoved the dollars she had left in her back pocket of her shorts.

"Oh no you don't," he tapped her on the shoulder. "Just answer me one question and I will leave you alone."

"Go on then", said Jasmine as she turned towards him with her arms folded closely to her chest.

"Why won't you give it a chance?" he asked.

"Because....well because, I'm too afraid to be honest. Been there, done that got the t-shirt and didn't like it. There, now have a good time. Thanks and all", Jasmine turned on her heel, waved and walked back to the hotel.

Spread eagle and face down on the bed, Jasmine soon dozed off. She was awoken by a gentle knocking and tapping on her hotel room door. She sat upright, cuddled her pillow to her chest and held her breath hoping whoever it was would go away. The knocking and tapping continued and in the end she gave in.

"Yes, who is it?"

"Jasmine, it's Julia, I met you earlier. Thought you could do with a friendly face right now".

"No, I'm okay thanks. Bye now", replied Jasmine as she crawled under the duvet and pulled it over her head.

"Well, I'm not going anywhere so you may as well open the door".

After the continual knocking, Jasmine kicked the duvet off, crawled off the bed and unlocked the door, then crawled back into bed. She didn't even look at Julia.

"I'm sorry about whaaat happened Jas. Thank gad the bomb didn't go off when you were in the jeep. Leo is mortified, I'll tell ya that for nothing", said Julia in her loud and high energy New York accent.

"Now get ya ass up and tawk to me".

Jasmine surfaced from under the cover with a face like a smacked backside.

"Julia, I'm not being funny or anything, but GO AWAY".

She marched to the bathroom and slammed the door.

"I ain't going nowhere" replied Julia as she blew bubbles with her bubble gum and proceeded to file her nails with an emery board that she had found in her handbag, whilst laying across the bed.

Jasmine sat on the edge of the bath, frustrated, hung over and wondering how to get rid of Julia. She pulled the white feather out of her shorts pocket, dropping the dollar bills all over the floor in the process, and stared at it for a while. Under her breath she muttered,

"What would Cerys do?"

An idea popped into her head. She decided that the only way she could get rid of Julia was to go to the party with her, act all normal as if she wanted to be there, then quietly slip out and slink off when no-one was watching.

"Cheers mate" she said to the feather as she climbed into the shower.

"That's my girl", shouted Julia as she heard the gushing sound of water emanating from the bathroom.

Jasmine mimicked her and said, "Mer mer mer, yada yada yada", childishly whilst rolling her eyes and grinning at her cunning plan.

Chapter 30

Dressed in her red, polka dot, vintage 1940s shirt swing, tea dress, Mary Jane stacked kitten heel pumps, Rita Hayworth hairstyle again and red lipstick, Jasmine looked the part.

"Wow wee, wuu woo, you look great", exclaimed Julia as she linked Jasmine's arm as they headed out of the hotel room.

Julia, who looked very elegant, slim and very tall, wore wide legged, ivory trousers, a silky fitted jade colour blouse that cinched into the waist and monochrome flat shoes. Her jet black hair was pinned up into a loose 'chignon' bun.

Jasmine took a deep breath as they walked into the large hall at the Diamond Head studio. It was packed full of actors, crew members, all film and TV industry people who had been involved in recreating the WWII productions. Julia showed their passes to security on the door. A 1940s swing band struck up the music "Little Brown Jug" as they entered the large hall that was decorated in American and Canadian flags. Also hoisted in the middle was the Hawaiian flag which Jasmine learned on her last visit to Hawaii, still displayed the Union Jack on it.

Above the band was a banner that read,

"Lest We Forget".

Some of the actors were still wearing their uniforms, others had decided to go for more of the casual look and some were wearing Hawaiian shirts. Julia, determined not to let go of Jasmine, guided her around the edge of the dance floor where some of the dancers were attempting the jive, the Lindy hop and the jitterbug, whilst others abandoned the 40s theme and were doing the robot moves and body popping.

Julia plonked Jasmine down on a seat at a table on her own and was commanded to, "Stay there", with a wagging finger.

Jasmine looked around the room. She saw Leo's mates at the bar but there was no sign of Leo. She felt disappointed but the little voice in her head kept saying,

"Be strong, fuck him and fuck them all. You are fine on your own".

She tapped her fingers on the table, biding her time to make her escape. Julia, Rainbow and a group of others suddenly appeared with a stack of glasses and a jug of beer. They sat down and poured each a glass. Rainbow smiled at her then turned and started nattering with Julia. The others also said hello but carried on talking amongst themselves. Jasmine felt invisible, lonely and totally pissed off.

She watched the dancers and drifted off into her own little world wondering what this evening would have been like if Leo hadn't gone all funny and left her. They would be dancing, having fun, he would hold her in his arms when the slow tunes were played. She suddenly snapped out of it when Rick and Joe approached the table and asked some of the girls to dance. The band were playing " Boogie Woogie Bugle Boy" and three female singers, dressed in army uniform, were singing in harmony in the background, to the music.

Rick took hold of Jasmine's hand, kissed it and winked at her.

"May I have the next dance ma'am", he said sweetly.

Jasmine smiled sarcastically at him and turned away.

The voice in her head couldn't be heard any more but the longing in her chest for Leo was overwhelming. She sipped her beer slowly, made small talk with the others on her table, when they remembered she was there, and stared aimlessly at the door.

"May I", said Rick insistently as he held out his hand to Jasmine.

"I'm not really in the mood, sorry", replied Jasmine. She just wanted to go back to her hotel room, climb into bed until it was time to catch her flight home. She felt completely and utterly hopeless.

Rick wouldn't take no for an answer. He took her drink from her hand, placed it on the table and lifted her out of her chair and carried her to the dance floor. The group at her table all clapped.

"Now they're interested", thought Jasmine to herself.

The band played 'Moonlight Serenade' as Rick held her closely. She tried to push him away but he wouldn't let go. He was really strong and gripped her tightly. She gave in and placed her head against his chest. She couldn't hold it any longer. Tears started to trickle down her cheeks. Rick held her even closer and caressed her neck softly as he started to gently manoeuvre her to the edge of the dance floor. Jasmine wiped her tears but kept her face turned into his chest, looking downwards at the floor. Unexpectedly he let go of her and Leo appeared in front of her. He took hold of Jasmine in his arms, lifted her chin up towards him and kissed her passionately. Her head was in a spin, her legs felt like jelly. He pulled her away from the dance floor into a quiet corner.

Even though his eyes were puffy and dewy and he stank of whiskey, she still fancied the ass off him. He was still in his uniform and his clean shaven chin had sprouted a sexy stubble.

"Jasmine, forgive me please. I'm so sorry. I was so scared. I ….."

"Shhhhush" said Jasmine, as she placed one finger on his lips to hush him.

"I know". She kissed him softly on the lips.

"I can't be without you. I really can't. Rick kicked my ass and made me see sense after he saw you today". He whispered as she clutched his body tightly. They talked and kissed and cried, not realizing that Leo's mates were watching closely.

"Right you two, you've had enough time to kiss and make up now come and join us", said Joe as he grabbed Leo's arm and lead him over to the table of onlookers.

"A toast", said Dylan. "To the memory of the fallen, the military past and present. Our gratitude and respect to them and their families and God bless those that continue to serve. Cheers".

"A toast", said Joe, who was extremely drunk and merry.

"I would like to make a toast to lying, stealing, cheating and drinking. If you are going to lie, lie for a friend. If you are going to steal, steal a heart. If you are going to cheat, cheat death and if you are going to drink, drink with me".

They all clinked their glasses and shouted, "Oorah".

Jasmine's fears and worries and confusion seemed to have washed away in the copious amount of beer she had been drinking, especially on top of her cocktail lunch. She felt carefree and very, very happy. She randomly, in her drunken state, kept kissing her feather that she had taken with her in her handbag and when Leo asked why, she replied it was one of Cerys' feathers from her angel wings. Something she wouldn't ordinarily say out loud in sober circumstances. Leo didn't understand but let her get on with it. As long as it made her happy he didn't care. It was getting late and some people had started to leave the party but Leo and Jasmine's crowd were still in full swing. A couple of the girls went up on stage and sang, "Chattanooga choo choo", along with the band. Every one stood up and clapped and sang along with them. Then Dylan and Rick joined them and sang, "Don't sit under the apple tree with anyone else but me". Everyone laughed at their attempts at becoming the Andrews sisters.

Jasmine decided she wanted to give it a go. All her inhibitions and insecurity seemed a thing of the past. She spoke with the band who nodded back at her. Leo shrugged his shoulders as he had no idea what she was going to sing.

"Right, Hiya everyone", she waved. "You probably don't know this song as it's a British one but my grandmother, who worked in a tank factory during the Second World War in Britain, taught me this. It's by Gracie Fields and it's about the women who had to work in factories with tools and machinery they had never used before and they didn't have a clue what they were called. She nodded at the band. Leo, Julia and Joe whistled.

Jasmine began quoting a song:

You've heard of Florence Nightingale,
Grace Darling and the rest,
You've all seen Greta Garbo
And her bosom friend, Mae West,
But there's a little lady, I want you all to meet
She's working on munitions and she lives just down the street.

She can't pretend to be, a great celebrity
But still... she's most important in her way,
The job she has to do, may not seem like much to you
But all the same, I'm very proud to say...

She began to sing:

She's the girl that makes the thing,
That drills the hole,
That holds the spring,
That drives the rod,
That turns the knob,
That works the thing-ummy-bob.

She's the girl that makes the thing,
That holds the oil,
That oils the ring,
That takes the shank
That moves the crank
That works the thing-ummy-bob.

It's a ticklish sort of job making a thing for a thing-ummy-bob especially when you don't know what it's for.

Jasmine spoke again:

*She's not what you would call,
A heroine, at all,
I don't suppose you'll even know her name
And though she'll never boast,
Of her important post
She strikes a blow for Britain just the same"*

She sang the chorus again.
Everyone joined in with her as she waved her arms around,

*But it's the girl
That makes the thing
That drills the hole
That holds the spring
That works the thing-ummy-bob
That makes the engines roar.*

*And it's the girl that makes the thing that holds the oil
That oils the ring that works the thing-ummy-bob
That's going to win the war.*

"I THANK YOU"

Jasmine was met with a standing ovation. Leo covered his face as he laughed so hard. He lifted her off the stage and shouted,
"I love you".

Everyone was still whistling and clapping and Jasmine shouted,

"What, I can't hear you".

"I LOVE YOU", he shouted again just as the next singer was making their way to the stage and the onlookers had begun to quieten down.

Everyone heard him and they all began to clap and whistle again.

Jasmine grinned from ear to ear. She pulled him in close and whispered,

"I love you too".

He led her off the dance floor and kissed her passionately. Joe approached them both, shook Leo's hand and kissed Jasmine on the cheek.

"She is a real keeper mate." Then he leaned into towards Leo and whispered, "and she is damn good at blowing a bugle too, and if she is good at blowing that... well... you are one lucky son of a gun, you know that right?" He winked. "How rude", she giggled.

Later that night, back at the hotel, they made mad, passionate, raw, intense enduring, animalistic, love, like never before.

Chapter 31

The lovers awoke late the next morning but hurriedly showered and dressed as Leo had promised Jasmine a proper American breakfast just like the ones she had at the Turtle Bay Resort. Both were still a little hung-over but both were ravenously hungry. They had both worked up quite an appetite. After a several coffees, fruit, pancakes with maple syrup, eggs and bacon, the couple took a stroll, hand in hand, to the beach. The air was cool and the sky was overcast with small strips of blue peeking through every now and then.

Christmas lights and decorations were everywhere and the sound of seasonal songs echoed around the stores.

"One and a half days left together," sighed Jasmine.

"I know but flights are cheap and regular off season so we'll make it work. Then after that we'll sort something, don't worry. Just take each day as it comes. We will be less than a day's flight away from each other", replied Leo as he kissed Jasmine on the top of her head.

"I know, but with work and stuff, it's going to be hard", she replied.

"Like I said, one day at a time okay," he smiled back.

They walked passed a group of surfers cleaning and waxing their boards when one called out to Jasmine,

"Hey ma'am, hello! You are back already? Must love it here huh? Where's your friend, the screaming one?" he laughed.

It was Koka, the waiter from the Luau that helped Cerys with her jellyfish sting.

"Hello, yes back again, can't keep away, it's too beautiful here", she tried to avoid the question about Cerys.

"It sure is ma'am. Your friend, not so fond of coming back then?" he grinned.

"Sadly, the young lady passed away, not long after returning home, she was very unwell", said Leo as he rescued Jasmine from having to say the words.

Koka stood up with a shocked expression on his face. He walked towards them both and stood in front of them.

"Oh, I am so so sorry. I hope I didn't upset you. My condolences. She was a lovely lady, very funny. So sorry."

"Oh, thank you, you are very kind", replied Jasmine as she clasped Leo's hand tightly.

Leo nodded.

"Come and join us at sunset here. We are having a paddle out and memorial service for a dear friend who passed tragically after a surfing accident, and in honour of all our fallen fellows. We can honour your friend as well. Please come", said Koka.

"Yes, go on then. I'll bring a blanket and we can sit and watch from here", said Jasmine.

Leo agreed.

"No, you must join us in the paddle out. The waves are low so it will be easy. We have plenty of boards and wet suits".

"Oh, I dunno. The last time I went on a surf board was when I was a teenager on holiday in Cornwall with my parents. I was only kneeling on it and I fell off and it almost knocked me out." said Jasmine, shaking her head.

"Yeah, I haven't surfed in years either", said Leo.

"Don't worry, we have all been surfing for ever", replied Koka as he pointed at his fellow surfers who were still waxing their boards.

"We'll take good care of you".

"Oh go on then, yes okay. Shall we meet here just before sunset then?" asked Jasmine warily.

Koka nodded. They shook hands, and waved at Koka's friends as they carried on with their walk.

"You serious about doing a paddle out?" laughed Leo.

"Aye, why not....for Cerys eh? I can imagine her laughing her tits off at the prospect of me clambering onto a surf board. What have we got to lose?"

"Dignity?" Leo replied.

The early evening arrived too quickly. The couple had be dreading it and looking forward to it at the same time. They met Koka and his surfing fellows on the beach, who provided them with wet suits and a surfboard each. The beach was packed with onlookers and surfers. The surfers started to make their way to the sea.

"Ready?" asked Koka as he placed a bunch of colourful leis over each of their heads and around each of their necks.

"Ready", said Leo and Jasmine in harmony. Koka stayed at Jasmine's side as they paddled out beyond the breakers. She was straddling the board and paddled with all her strength. Leo was a little in front of her. Calvin, Koka's surfing buddy, mentored him through the breakers. Once they were beyond the waves, paddling became a little easier. The cold, dark, blue ocean was calm. The sun had begun to set reflecting its orange glows over the darkness. The sinking sun turned the ocean to liquid gold.

There must have been over one hundred surfers in the sea that evening. They had straddled their boards and paddled out to form a huge circle. Jasmine, Leo, Koka and Calvin joined them. Everyone joined hands in union and solidarity. Jasmine thought it felt very spiritual and electric. Koka told them to copy him and the others. Everyone started to splash the water with clasped hands and then chants, and whistles were sent into the open sky to remember those that had passed.

"Bless you and miss you Cerys", whispered Jasmine as she looked up at the sky.

Leis, wreaths and loose flowers were thrown into the centre of the circle, followed by a few moments of silence. Finally, the surfers pointed their boards to the sky and slowly turned towards the shore with the flowers swirling in their wake behind them. Calvin and Koka helped to guide Jasmine and Leo safely back to shore.

"Wow that was incredible, thank you for inviting us", said Jasmine as she rubbed her wet hair with a towel and slid out of her wet suit displaying her pert nipples under her bikini top.

"Yep, that was pretty damn amazing", said Leo as he shook Koka and Calvin's hand.

"You are most welcome. It was lovely to see you both. Come back soon. Take care now", replied Koka as he gathered up the couples surfboards and wets suits and headed towards the surfboard shack at the end of the beach.

"Yep, same here", said Calvin as he walked up the beach aiding Koka.

"Thank you", they both shouted after the surfers as they pulled on their clothes.

"That was electrifying wasn't it?" said Leo as they made their way back to the hotel, "and there's more to come", he grinned.

"Go on, tell me what it is...pleeeease", begged Jasmine.

The night was still young so the couple hurried back to the hotel to shower and change. Leo had organised something special for their final evening and Jasmine was dying to know what it was. He had booked it last minute whilst she was getting ready that morning.

A taxi was waiting for them outside. After a short journey they arrived at Waikiki beach. Leo grabbed Jasmine's hand and hotfooted it towards a twin hulled, forty foot catamaran that was waiting on the edge of the beach.

"Hurry up or they will go without us", said Leo.

The crew helped them on board and welcomed them with a glass of champagne as they set sail. It was just the two of them and the crew and no-one else. Leo had hired the catamaran for a few hours. Jasmine was overwhelmed.

"This is wonderful, aw thank you", she said as she kissed him a million times around his forehead, cheeks and chin and of course, his lips.

"We were supposed to be here before sunset but the paddle out seemed to good a thing to miss so I called the boat hire company to rearrange it, is that okay".

"Okay? It's bloody brilliant mun", she laughed.

They enjoyed a two course dinner of Hawaiian Kalua pork with bok choy and to follow, coconut pie with ice cream for dessert, washed down with a large bottle of champagne.

"As night draws nearer the cityscape of Honolulu and Waikiki along with the famous crater of Diamond Head and the Ko'olau Mountains will become a beautiful silhouette," said one of the crew members as he showed them the shore.

"Wow", said the couple in tandem.

"Thank you Leo, this is so wonderful." said Jasmine as she sat on his lap and kissed him for the millionth time.

The cruise lasted a couple of hours as planned and as the crew turned the catamaran back towards Waikiki beach they stopped for a while to take in the view of the spectacular fireworks from the Hilton Hawaiian Village. The stunning array of colours lit up the sky over Waikiki. Leo watched Jasmine's face as she watched the colourful show in awe. She turned to find him down on one knee.

"Oh my God, what are you doing", said Jasmine.

"Jasmine, marry me...please", said Leo as he produced a white gold single diamond engagement ring from his shirt pocket.

"Um, oh God, YES...YES", said Jasmine jumping up and down like Tigger.

Leo grabbed her and steadied her in case she tipped the boat over.

"I love you beautiful", he said as she kissed her passionately.

"Congratulations", shouted the crew from behind them.

"Oops, I almost forgot they were there", laughed Jasmine.

Back at the hotel, they celebrated in their usual way.....in bed....making love!

After the euphoria had settled down they tried to discuss how their engagement was going to work with him living in Canada and her living in Wales. Leo hadn't really thought it through. When he came to his senses about their relationship, just before the 1940s party, he went and bought a ring on the way there...just like that. No forward planning or forethought at all. He had no idea how he was going to propose to her until he saw a brochure in the hotel lobby about hiring a boat and liked the idea.

They finally decided to try and see each other as much as possible with flights over when they were not working. Leo would ask his agent to see if she could get him some acting jobs in the UK to start with at least. He was off work over Christmas so he planned to stay with Jasmine and Jasmine would go to Canada for a few days over the New Year's holidays. Time would be tight but they were determined to give it a go.

The time had come for them to go their separate ways, for a short time anyway. It was a tearful but joyful time at the airport as Leo waved Jasmine off. His flight was a few hours later than hers. He had planned to meet up with some of the other actors that were still left on the island for a farewell drink first. All the way home Jasmine admired her engagement ring and secretly talked to her feather when no-one was looking!!

Chapter 32

Christmas and New Year came and went. Steve took everyone to The Mumbles in the Gower on Christmas Eve to scatter Cerys' ashes. It was her favourite time of the year and her favourite place to go as a child. Steph met them there as well. It was a sad moment for all of them but it was a great get together at the same time.

Jasmine was slowly running out of leave to take from work. Leo travelled over when he could and any time they weren't together they spoke on the phone or via Skype. Olivia and Alex were surprised but happy about the engagement. Steph was over the moon and demanded to be bridesmaid when the happy event arrived.

Olivia and Steve had become quite close since Cerys' funeral and had started dating. Steph and Maria had also started to see a lot of each other as well. Romance was in the air all around, except for Alex. He was happy to play the field and have a girl in each town.

Leo's agent managed to get him an acting job in Bristol in the theatre production, "To kill a Mockingbird" for two weeks and then eight days straight after in the theatre production,

"Peter James', The Perfect Murder" in the New Theatre in Cardiff during the spring.

"Jasmine, Steve and I want to invite you, Leo and Alex for dinner Saturday night at my house. We have something to discuss. Ring me back to confirm you are coming", played the answer machine as Jasmine checked her messages after a long shift at work. She had not found it easy working at the police station over the last few months. Her colleagues were great but it was just some of the people they had to deal with over the counter and on the phone. Some of them were just so downright rude and ignorant. That day she had to deal with an angry man, called Thomas Thomas, who had series hygiene problems and hardly any teeth which made his speech difficult to understand, demanding that he had his air rifles back. They were seized by the firearms department after he had threatened to shoot his neighbour. Jasmine explained that the firearms department would contact him once they had finished their investigations and there was nothing she could do other than contact them on his behalf to say he had been in to ask for them back. It was out of her hands. After his rant he left the station shouting that he was going to complain to the Chief Constable about it, to which Jasmine replied,

"Have a magical day Mr Thomas", in a sarcastic manner.

Later that day the Local Neighbourhood Police Commander's Business manager Eliza rang Jasmine to say that the Chief Constable's secretary had contacted her to say a man with impeded speech, by the name of Thomas Thomas, had rang her saying his local station won't give him his 'Pelicans' back and he wants to talk to the Chief. She tried to ask him what he meant but he kept asking for his 'Pelicans'. He became so frustrated in her querying his request, he hung up on her.

After a lot of giggling, Jasmine explained about Mr Thomas having had his air rifles seized. He was asking for his pellet guns back. Eliza the Business manager thought it was hilarious and rang the Chief's secretary to let her know. "That's going to have to go in next week's General Orders" she laughed.

Jasmine, Leo, Alex, Olivia and Steve were sat around the table at Olivia's house enjoying a homemade chicken curry that Steve had cooked.

"So what's this thing we have to discuss then mum", asked Jasmine whilst scooping up some curry sauce and rice with a piece of naan bread.

"Well, me and Steve, that is....Steve and I... have decided to move in together. We are not getting any younger and we really enjoy each other's company. It seems daft to keep running two houses when I am either staying over at his house or he is staying at mine. What do you think?"

They all agreed it would be a great idea.

"I hope this doesn't change my inheritance gran", laughed Alex as he helped himself to more curry.

"I shall cut you off altogether young man if you keep being cheeky to me like that" she said jokingly as she tapped him on the back of his hand with a spoon.

"Oww...sorry gran. Just Joking I am".

"I know you are my little choochy oochy face", said Olivia as she pulled his face towards her and squeezed his cheeks together.

"Liv stopped teasing the poor lad", said Steve.

"Oh, she's allowed you to call her Liv has she", laughed Jasmine.

"Can I call you that too", asked Leo.

"You can call me whatever you want sweetheart, within reason" said Olivia.

"Well go on, tell them the rest of it", said Steve as he nudged Olivia.

"There's more?" asked Alex.

"Well, it's just an idea, nothing definite yet. Steve and I are thinking of selling both of our houses and moving nearer the Gower coast. Steve is going to retire and hand his business over to his nephew, Rhys."

"Go on", said Jasmine, intrigued by what was coming next.

"Well, we thought that maybe you would like to sell your house as well, and we could pool the money that we make between us into a tidy sized house so we could all live there together. We have seen a beautiful house with five bedrooms, two bathrooms, a holiday cottage in the grounds and a pool. It also has a few acres of land surrounding it. We thought we would build and open a boarding kennels there. We thought that with you and Leo flitting back and fore across the Atlantic, it would be easier. Ruby and Bridget would no longer have to be packed off to kennels every time you go away, we could look after them. Alex can have his own room and bathroom in the main house when he is home from University and you and Leo can have the holiday cottage as your own. What do you think?" asked Olivia.

"Blimey, that's a lot to take in. What about my job though. It's a long way to travel from the Gower every day?" said Jasmine.

"Well we've thought about that. You're not happy doing that job are you and quite frankly we worry about you working there, having to deal with vile people all the time, so we thought that maybe you could help out in the kennels when you are here. You will have plenty of money from the sale of the house to keep you going for a while as well. We've worked it all out, here are the figures. My solicitor has checked it all out and agrees it's a good idea, as long as you think it is", said Steve. "We'll have it all drawn up fairly between us so no one loses out on their inheritance", he laughed whilst ruffling Alex's hair.

"Sounds like a fantastic idea. My folks have a large house back home so we could do the same there and sell my house too. I would have to ask them though. It would save my Mom having to go around and check on it every time I'm here in England I mean Wales", said Leo as Jasmine kicked him under the table.

So that's what they did. They opened a kennels and moved into the large house in the Gower. Jasmine gave up her job at the police station. She had four leaving parties all in all as she had worked with so many people over the years and they couldn't all go at the same time because of different shift patterns, hence the four leaving doos.

Jasmine and Leo finally married in a small ceremony in Rhossili in Wales, with Steph and Maria as their bridesmaids, and spent their honeymoon in Canada with Leo's family and friends. Leo landed a lead role in a Zombie movie in the USA and he also had a regular spot in a British sit com. They heard nothing more about Astrid or Lukas and they didn't want to know, in all honesty....to be fair....to be honest.

Olivia and Steve didn't marry but they loved each other's company, they were inseparable. Their boarding kennels was a great success and they had bookings all year round.

Alex went on to gain a first class honours in his degree and went to work for an animation company in

London. Leo did a voice over for one of the characters Alex designed for a short animation film. They had great fun recording it.

Steph and Maria married in a civil ceremony in Wales and went on to have twins, a girl and a boy, after having IVF treatment. The girl was named Cerys and the boy was Morgan, or Mog as they called him.

Molly, Lucy, Aiden, Ginger and Mickey won half a million pound each in a lottery syndicate they had between them a year later. They also gave up their jobs at the police station. Molly retired and she and her husband Gerry went on lots of holidays, Aiden and his wife Kay bought a boat and went sailing around the Mediterranean, Lucy and her husband Marc bought a farm, and both Ginger and Mickey retired and helped out their families.

The white feather that Jasmine found on the beach in Hawaii stayed with her always. At quiet times, she would sit and talk to it. Leo always said to her if anyone ever saw her doing that, she would be carted off to the funny farm. He understood though, and on the rare occasion Jasmine had caught him talking to it as well.

She knew it was daft but it was a comfort for her. She believed that Cerys was her Guardian Angel and that the feather belonged to her. She believed that Cerys had sent it to her to so that she knew she was watching over her.

The end.

****

Well, if this was the end of a film, all the cast and crew (and the writer) would be holding hands singing, "We'll meet again".

Then as the credits role, all the cast and crew, and the writer, would take part in a flash mob dancing production to the song "Twist and Shout", in the John Lewis shopping Centre in Cardiff, just to round it off.... why not!

Thank you for taking the time to read my story. I hope you enjoyed it. If you can't afford to live your dream, write about it and escape from reality. It's good for the heart, mind, body and soul.

In the words of Captain Sensible, and from the musical,

'South Pacific',

"You've got to have a dream, if you don't have a dream, how you gonna have a dream come true".

****

Just one more thing.....I hope you don't mind......

"What it is.... the day in the life of a Police Staff Station Enquiry Officer"

"What it is...." said the girl at the desk,

And so did the man with a tattoo and a vest.

"Sort out my life" demanded a woman with a moustache,

"I've been called a witch on Face book, what are you going to do about that?"

"It's probably right", one thought in silence as the woman carried on moaning about a man in a Robin Reliant.

Next came the man who had lost his wallet,

Smelly, unwashed with a greasy mullet.

"I need a police reference number to give to the social, and they will give me more dosh to spend down my local".

"What it is...." they came and went,

And on the phone they didn't relent.

"What it is...." from morning til night,

Until at last we turn off the light".

Night night, God bless. Xx

About the author

Samantha Ashdown was born in Newport, Gwent in the mid to late swinging sixties. She has worked for many years in a civilian support staff role within her local Police Force, firstly in the Force Control Room before moving out to her local police station working on the front counter, in the role of a Station Enquiry Officer.

She is divorced and has a grown up son, a very old collie cross dog and a tortoiseshell cat who is also a pensioner; and they all live happily in the luscious green and rolling hills of the South Wales Valleys.

"What it is..." is her first novel, although she has been writing short stories and poems in her rare spare time since she was at school. She started to write "What it is..." just over three years ago when she was home on sick leave from work after having a knee operation. She has started to write a sequel and is thoroughly enjoying doing it. It's her therapy and escapism after a hard long week at work.

Acknowledgements

My heartfelt thanks to my beautiful mum and my wonderful son who have supported me in everything I have done, through good times and hard times and who inspire me and push me on to keep going, no matter what...love you both with all my heart.

Thank you to all my friends, family, work colleagues, not forgetting 'Old' B relief FCR and my 'Canadian Crush', the actor Scott Gibson, who gave me the inspiration for the character Leo McKenzie.

Thank you to the makers of the WWII TV mini-series 'Band of Brothers' and 'The Pacific' that I watched when I was on sick leave and gave me some ideas and inspiration to write my novel.

Thanks to all the Hawaiian websites, holiday brochures and travel companies, TV shows about the islands that have provided me with all the information I needed as I've never been there so couldn't recount from experience.

A huge thanks again to my Mum, my brother Justin, Chris, Michelle, Ceri, Alexa, Rhian and Tania, my guinea pigs, for reading and wading through my very first draft, providing me with advice notes, and then for giving me a thumbs up afterwards. I would like to acknowledge Clare, a fighter and strong woman who has had more trials and tribulations within her family than any person I have ever known.

I would like to acknowledge by brother and my sister-in-law, Justin and Elaine and their grandchild Lee for their difficult times. Sleep in peace Michael.

Thanks to my close work colleagues for allowing me to use them as characters in my novel and adapting their characteristics and sayings. Again a huge thanks to my son Ben for helping me with the computer technology side of things.

I would like to thank PC Amie Holland from Greater Manchester Police for allowing me to use and adapt her powerful poem.

I would also like to acknowledge the front line police staff, front line police officers and our armed forces, present and past and the fallen, who protect and preserve us day in and day out.

"Lest we forget".

God bless you all.
(Gran, if you are watching over me, I miss you).

Thank you for choosing to read my novel.

Big cwtches and hugs to one and all.

Printed in Great Britain
by Amazon